DEAR ANNE...

A STORY OF PERSEVERANCE

TAMMY L BROWN

ISBN : 979-8-8689-3107-9

For all persecuted for their heritage and religion. I hear you and I will tell your stories in the hopes that humanity and compassion will live on.

PROLOGUE

"Dear Anne,

I don't even know where to start, Anne. It's so hard to find words for what happened today. I wish I could say this diary entry is filled with hope and happiness, but it's the opposite. It's darkness and despair. I'm sitting here in this cold, damp safe room beneath the kibbutz, clutching your diary in one hand and wiping away my tears with the other. You, Anne, are my only source of comfort right now, my only confidante in this world turned upside down.

It all started with the sirens blaring again, just like the ones you described in your diary. I grabbed my little brother, Yoni, and ran as fast as I could toward the safe room, my heart pounding like crazy. The air was filled with the shrieks of the rockets overhead, and the world seemed to explode around us.

We reached the entrance of the safe room, and I could hear Mama's voice shouting at me to hurry. I was almost there, Anne, so close to safety. But then it happened. A deafening explosion, a blinding flash of light, and everything changed.

I turned for a split second, Anne, and I saw it all: the fire, the smoke, the chaos. I saw Yoni, my sweet two-year-old brother, being thrown through the air like a rag doll, his tiny body consumed by flames. I screamed, Anne, I screamed with all my might, but it was as if the world had gone mute. I saw my little brother die, and there was nothing I could do. The image is burned into my mind, and I can't escape it.

I made it into the safe room, Anne, but only me, and I can't shake off the guilt. If only I had been faster, if only I had held onto him tighter, maybe he would still be here. The world can be so cruel, Anne, and it feels like

it's taken away the one person I loved most
in this world.

I don't know where Mama, Papa, and Daniel
are. I don't know if they made it to safety or if
they're out there in the chaos. Right now, I'm
alone in this dimly lit room, surrounded by
concrete walls. And the only solace I have is
this diary, your diary, where you wrote about
your own experiences in such a different, yet
strangely similar time.

I want to believe that someday, this madness
will end, and my family will be reunited. But
right now, Anne, all I can think about is
Yoni, and how his innocent life was taken
away so brutally. I wish I could hold him
one more time, feel his tiny fingers wrapped
around mine, and tell him how much I love
him.

Thank you, Anne, for listening to me. Writing
to you feels like a lifeline in these dark days.
I hope that someday when the storm has

passed, I can look back on this entry and
remember that even in the darkest of times,
there was a glimmer of hope, a connection
with you, a friend who understands the pain
I'm going through.

Yours,

Rachel"

CHAPTER I

The blasts shake me from my sleep, my heart hammering as I sit up. The room is still dark, dawn only a promise outside my haven. Another explosion sounds in the distance, the rattle and boom are familiar now. I shiver, pulling my blanket tight around my shoulders. My bare feet find the cold floor. I'm thirteen today, but I don't feel like celebrating.

I shuffle to the broken mirror, peering at my reflection. My brown waves are a tangled mess, hazel eyes wide with fear. I hear shouts outside, orders barked in Hebrew. The gunfire is constant now, bullets zinging through the air. I flinch with every shot, shoulders hunched.

I'm alone here, separated from my parents during the raids from Hamas. We came seeking refuge but found only more war. Now it's just me in this little room, the explosions, my unwanted company. I wish I could see my best friend Yael again, hear her whisper secrets, and giggle with me through the night. Instead, all I have is the shelling, and rockets screeching overhead.

I sit on my thin mattress, listening. The sounds of battle used to make me cry, but now I just feel numb. I am hollow inside, like a scooped-out melon. I take out my diary, its pages are my only comfort now.

"Dear Anne,"

I write with a shaking hand,

"It's my birthday today..."

I stare at the blank page, pen poised but frozen. Where do I even begin? So much has happened since we came here, so much fear and loss.

"Another explosion rocks the walls, closer this time."

I whimper, gripping my pen tighter.

"Anne, I wish you were here with me. Your words and courage give me hope, even in the darkest days. I read your diary repeatedly, taking comfort in your voice. Now I need that comfort more than ever.

The gunfire is constant, bullets ripping through the air outside. I cringe with each shot, shoulders hunched against the sounds. Booms and rattling bursts punctuate the shouts of soldiers, their voices muffled by the walls. But nothing can mute the explosions when they come.

All I have is your diary and these pages, daring me to write the awful truths I have seen.

Another blast shakes the walls, dust raining down. I cough, eyes burning.

"Oh, Anne, I am so scared."

The battle rages on outside, but I am trapped here within. My hands tremble as I write, thoughts scattered.

"Please stay with me, Anne. I need your light to face the dark.

Yours always,

Rachel"

The pounding of my heart fills the silence between explosions. I pause, listening, pen hovering over the page. Any second the door could burst open, soldiers spilling in. Would they be friend or foe? I don't know anymore. Allegiances blur, in a war until only survival matters.

"I wish I could see my parents' faces again and touch the warmth of their skin. Do they still live? Are they safe?"

My empty stomach growls, but I scarcely notice.

"Hunger is an old friend now. What I crave most is the comfort of their arms, the gentle rumble of Papa's laughter.

Mama's voice soothes me as I imagine it, her lullabies floating through the darkness. I see her tired smile as she smooths back my hair, the creases around her eyes deepening. 'Be strong, my love,' she whispers. 'We'll be together soon.' I cling to those words, playing them on repeat in my mind.

The waiting stretches on, minutes bleed into hours. Sometimes I doze, slumped against the hard wall. But sleep brings no respite, only twisting dreams filled with fire and screaming. I startle awake, heart hammering. The explosions continue, as the world is upended outside my tiny haven.

When will it end, Anne? How much longer can we endure?"

I fill page after page, writing until my hand cramps, just to hear your voice in my mind.

"You give me courage, even now. I will not give up, I promise you. Someday we will both be free.

Yours in hope,

Rachel"

The blasts thunder on, shaking the very walls around me. I huddle in the corner, knees drawn to my chest. Each explosion makes me flinch, imagining the destruction raining down overhead. Are people dying up there? Homes crumbling, lives ruined in an instant.

"Dear Anne,

I long to see the sun again, to feel its warmth on my face. Down here in the dark, time loses meaning. My thoughts turn to Yael, with her fiery hair and ready laugh. Is she trapped somewhere like me, waiting for the all-clear signal that never comes? Or did she try to run to safety, only to be cut down by a hail of bullets?

I cannot let myself think that way. Yael has always been a survivor, resourceful and quick. Surely, she found a way out when the air raid sirens screamed. She is probably in a safe room like this one, scribbling in her own diary to pass the endless hours underground.

We will have so much to tell each other when we finally reunite, spinning stories late into the night like we used to. I imagine us collapsed in giggles, faces flushed. The war will seem far away then.

For now, I steady my breathing and let my mind drift to happier times. I think of walking hand-in-hand with Mama through the kibbutz, greeting neighbors at each little

house. I remember plucking oranges right
from the tree, juice running down my chin.

Those memories sustain me, even as the world
above rages on. I will see the sunshine again.
I will.

With hope,

Rachel"

"Dear Anne,

The air down here is stale and heavy. I feel it
settling into my lungs with each breath,
making my chest tight. The bombs have
stopped for now, but the echoing booms still
ring in my ears. I am curled up on a thin
mattress in the corner, a single lightbulb

casting harsh shadows across the concrete walls.

Writing in this diary is the only thing keeping me sane. As I spill my innermost thoughts onto these pages, I can almost pretend you are here listening, your kind eyes urging me on. How I wish I could truly speak with you, wise Anne. You would know just what to say to calm my racing mind.

Up above, I know the world is burning. Plumes of smoke darken the skies day and night. I haven't seen the sun in what feels like forever. Sometimes I wonder if it still exists at all.

Mama's face floats through my memory – her warm smile, her gentle voice. Is she out there searching for me amidst the rubble and ruin? My heart aches to see her again. I hope with everything in me that she and Papa made it to safety when the air raid sirens sounded. They must be alright; they just must be.

I cling to the belief that someday soon this war will end. Someday I will breathe fresh air and see flowers blooming once more. I will run freely through the kibbutz and play hide and seek with Yael behind the big oak tree. I will sit with Mama and Papa beneath the stars, feeling at peace.

This darkness cannot last forever. Light always returns in the end.

With weary hope,

Rachel"

"Dear Anne,

The minutes crawl by in this cramped safe room. It has been hours since I've heard any sounds besides my own breathing. I am not even sure if anyone else made it here.

It is so quiet. Too quiet.

I long to hear Yael's infectious laugh or Papa's deep, calming voice. My ears strain for any sign of life outside these cold concrete walls. But there is only silence.

I am alone.

At first, the solitude felt like a refuge, a rare moment of peace in the chaos. Now it closes in on me, suffocating in its totality. I have never felt so isolated, so cut off from everything and everyone I love.

My thoughts spiral as the minutes turn to hours. Are they even looking for me? Do they think I am already gone? Have they fled for safety, leaving me behind?

I want to cry out, to break this smothering silence. But I stay frozen, too afraid to make a sound. The smallest noise could alert the enemies prowling above. I cannot risk it.

So, I will wait here, alone, straining my ears for any hint of hope. My heart races as I face the bitter truth – I may be trapped in this isolation forever. Still, a flicker of faith remains inside me. I must cling to it with all I have left.

Anne, please stay with me. I need your strength now more than ever.

With waning hope,

Rachel"

CHAPTER II

My heart pounded against my chest when I first burst through the hidden door and slammed it shut behind me. The gunshots still echo in my ears, drowning out the screams that ring in my head. I am sitting down against the cold, concrete wall, still struggling to catch my breath. My hands tremble uncontrollably as the image of my baby brother's lifeless body flashes before my eyes repeatedly.

Why? Why did this happen? I bury my face in my hands as a sob racks my body. I want to scream, but no sound comes out. The terror grips me like a vice, squeezing the air from my lungs. I am helpless, powerless. My brother is gone and there is nothing I can do.

I hug my knees to my chest, making myself as small as possible in the tiny room. The gunfire outside continues in sporadic bursts. Each shot makes me flinch. I want to block it out, but the sounds penetrate the thick walls, echoing all around me. Nowhere is safe.

Silent tears stream down my face as my mind races. How long until they find me here? How long until I am next? I rock slowly back and forth, the movement calming my frayed nerves ever so slightly. But the fear remains coiled inside me like a snake, ready to strike again at any moment. I take a shaky breath, trying to slow my pounding heart. I just need to survive one moment at a time.

I need something to hold onto, something to keep me grounded amidst this nightmare.

My eyes fall upon an old familiar friend in the corner. Anne's diary. My hands tremble as I reach for the worn little book, its pages creased and faded from years of reading. As my fingers brush over the familiar cover, some of the tension in my body releases. Opening to a random page, Anne's words soothe me like a lullaby:

"I don't think of all the misery, but of the beauty that still remains." (Frank, 1991)

Tears fill my eyes, blurring the ink on the page. My dear friend Anne understands. Even in her own darkest days, locked away from the world, she found light. Anne suffered so much, yet never lost her spirit. She gives me hope.

Clutching the diary to my chest, I breathe deeply for the first time since fleeing to this room. Anne's words are a lifeline, reminding me that beauty still exists beyond these walls, beyond this war. I am not alone. Anne's voice lifts me, soothing my soul when I need it most.

Though she lived decades ago, it feels as if she sits beside me, her gentle wisdom calming my storms. I brush my fingers over the faded cover once more, drawing strength from her words. With Anne beside me, I can face the darkness.

I open my diary; the pages are still crisp and new. My hands tremble as I poise my pen over the blank page. Who will read these words when I'm gone? Will my diary survive like Anne's, or will it turn to ash like so much else in this war?

I push the dark thoughts away. This diary is my refuge, the one place I can be honest. Taking a deep breath, I begin again:

"Dear Anne,

The air is thick with smoke today. It seeps under the door, stinging my eyes and burning my throat. I huddle here in the dark while chaos reigns outside. Some days this room feels like a sanctuary. Other days, like a tomb.

My life was so ordinary just days ago. School, friends, crushes – my biggest worries were homework and pimples. Now I wake each morning unsure if I'll see the sunset. Food is scarce, water is rationed, and my body is in a constant state of hunger and thirst. I never knew such suffering existed.

Yet even amidst the rubble, moments of beauty remain. A shard of broken glass catching a glimpse of sunshine, the full moon shining through the smoke. A child's laughter drifts on the wind. These tiny miracles sustain me, just as your words do.

We are kindred spirits, you and me. Both hidden away as war rages around us. Both seeking comfort in scribbled words. Both straining to hear songbirds over screeching bombs.

I hope with all my heart this war will end, and that I'll live to feel the sun on my face again. But if not, I want the world to know my story, just as we know yours. Let my words be a light in the darkness, as yours have been for me.

With hope,

Rachel"

"Dear Anne,

The air in this room grows stagnant and stale, heavy with the scent of my unwashed body and festering wounds. I ration every drop of water, every morsel of food.

My stomach gnaws at itself, my tongue like sandpaper in my parched mouth.

During the day, I maintain strict silence. Any noise could give away my hiding spot if the soldiers sweep through. I strain to hear snippets of the world outside - shouts, explosions, screams. At night, the gunfire is relentless. Tracer rounds split the sky, rockets whistle overhead. I cover my ears, but the sounds pierce through.

My dreams provide no respite. I relive the day they came for us over and over. The pounding at the door, Mama's panic, the soldiers forcing their way inside. Dragging us from our home. The cracks of rifles splitting the air, bodies dropping lifeless to the ground. I jolted awake gasping, soaked in sweat.

I have so little food left. Each bite is carefully rationed but I am always hungry. My face grows gaunt, and my ribs protrude. I run my fingers over the sharp edges of bone. Will I waste away in this room, my life reduced to mere survival? I cling to memories of better times, but they grow hazy, like a faded photograph.

I envy the innocence of my childhood. Back then I took peace for granted. Now it is all I yearn for. My kingdom for one more ordinary day. A hot meal, a warm bed, my family together once more. Simple joys that once seemed unremarkable now feel like distant dreams.

I must stay strong, Anne. For them. My words are now their legacy.

Yours in solidarity,

Rachel"

I grasp the diary tightly as more explosions rock the walls. The pen shakes in my hand but I will not stop writing. Each word is a small act of defiance. A refusal to be silenced.

"Dear Anne,

Do you remember what it was like, huddled away in darkness while the world raged outside? Did you feel as alone as I do in this moment? I wish I could ask you, speak with you beyond these pages. You would understand.

The waiting is interminable. Seconds crawl by. I strain to hear any sign the fighting has ended but only hear more blasts. I want to scream in frustration but stay silent, frozen. I envy the ignorant who sleep through this nightmare unaware.

My back aches feeling the hard floor through the paper thin mattress. The single bulb flickers, making shadows dance along the walls. I rub my arms, shivering, though sweat still clings to me. In this cramped space, my imagination runs wild. Each small sound magnifies into impending doom.

I must calm myself. Focus on my breath like Papa taught me. Inhale for five counts, exhale for five. Again. The knot in my chest loosens slightly.

Writing helps ease my mind too. I confess my deepest thoughts on these pages. Fears I bury rise to the surface. Here I can be vulnerable, break down, and fall apart. Then collect the pieces and carry on.

You give me strength, Anne. As long as I hold the pen, I have a purpose. I will tell our story.

Yours in solidarity,

Rachel"

I take a deep breath and open Anne's diary once more. The worn binding cracks gently as I flip through the pages. Her eloquent words soothe me and transport me from this harsh reality.

I read passages at random, snippets that resonate in this moment:

"I don't think of all the misery but of the beauty that still remains." (Frank, 1991)

"Think of all the beauty still left around you and be happy." (Frank, 1991)

I pause, blinking back tears.

"Dear Anne,

Your eternal optimism astounds me, even after enduring such horrors firsthand. I wish I had your courage."

Running my fingers over the faded ink, I make a silent vow. I will not succumb to fear or despair. Each day I will find beauty—in an act of kindness, a bloom pushing through rubble, a child's laughter.

I will cling to hope, as you did. Hope for an end to the violence, for a return to normalcy, however distant it seems. Hope is what sustains us. It lives inside these pages and within me. I only need to unleash it.

Tomorrow I will wake up and begin anew. I will open this diary and write, releasing my thoughts, and finding solace. We will get through this dark time as you did, dear Anne. One day at a time.

With admiration,

Rachel"

CHAPTER III

I sit alone in the hidden room, clutching my diary tightly to my chest. My heart pounds against my ribs, a rapid staccato fueled by fear and uncertainty. I take a deep, shaky breath, steeling myself to confront the reality that waits outside this sanctuary.

With trembling fingers, I open the diary to a fresh, blank page. The paper stares up at me, empty and accusing. I hesitate, overwhelmed by the task of putting words to the chaos in my mind.

In the distance, a burst of gunfire shatters the heavy silence. I flinch, goosebumps prickling my skin. The sound fades, but the echo remains, ringing in my ears.

My breaths come faster now, ragged and harsh in the enclosed space. I force air into my lungs, willing my heart to slow its frantic pace. In and out. In and out.

Finally, I take up my pen, its familiar weight steadying me. I begin to write, the words flow slowly at first, then gaining momentum. I address each entry to my hero, my kindred spirit across time and space. Anne Frank.

"Dear Anne,

The gunfire never stops. Day and night it crackles and booms, the soundtrack of my imprisonment..."

I pause, listening to the ominous rumble of rockets in the distance.

"How can this be happening again? Our people, persecuted, driven from their homes, and forced to cower in the darkness. Has the world learned nothing?"

My hand trembles as I write, emotions swirling within me. Fear, most of all. It stalks my every moment, stealing sleep, and haunting dreams.

"I am afraid to leave this room, afraid of what I'll find outside. Afraid the violence will consume everything if I don't keep it out.

But I cannot hide here forever. I know that, deep down. Like you, Anne, I must find the courage to face the darkest parts of humanity. To bear witness, even as my heart breaks.

Your words give me hope. In them, I find a kindred spirit who understands this fear. You weathered such evil but never lost faith. Your diary was a light in the darkness. I hope mine can be the same.

For now, it is my refuge. Here, I pour out my anguish, my longing for peace. Here, I find sanity amidst the madness. I do not know what comes next, but I will continue writing. My pen is mightier than their weapons."

I stop and read over the words. My hands have steadied, and my breathing slowed. I feel your presence, Anne, guiding

me. Giving me strength. This diary is my lifeline. As long as
I can write, I can endure.

I nod, taking a deep breath before continuing:

"The images haunt me – people fleeing in
terror as rockets rain down. I run with them,
stumbling through choking dust. Screams and
cries surround me, but I cannot stop.
Survival instinct takes over. I don't know
how I made it here, to the hidden room inside
the basement.

Now I sit alone, isolated. I long to see my
family, to know they are safe. But the heavy
door stays shut. I cannot risk being found.

Anne, were you this afraid in your hidden
annex? Did your heart also thunder in your
chest? I think of you now, finding comfort in
our shared experience. Two girls on the brink
of womanhood, robbed of our futures.

But not our voices. Our words endure, echoing across time. Yours inspired me in childhood; now mine will inspire others. I will write of humanity's resilience and our refusal to be defeated by darkness.

For as long as I can hold a pen, I will write. These pages are my refuge, my only escape from the nightmare around me. Here, I process my fear and grief. Here, I cling to hope.

Your spirit gives me courage, Anne. Because of you, I know - as long as I can write, I will survive. My diary, like yours, will be a light cutting through the darkness."

With trembling hands, I open to a fresh page. The familiar lines comfort me and ground me amidst the chaos.

I begin again:

"Dear Anne,

The gunfire started at dawn today. I awoke to pops and cracks, first distant then drawing closer. My heart seized in my chest. I wanted to melt into the sheets and disappear.

By breakfast, the kibbutz was under siege. We could see the trucks approaching and feel the ground shake with every shell. I watched my father's face turn ashen, though he tried to mask his fear. 'It's going to be okay,' he said, but his eyes betrayed him.

The day blurred into panicked fragments after that. Screams and smoke. Bodies rushed past, bloodied. I caught glimpses of familiar faces contorted in terror. My only clear memory is of my mother's hands clutching mine, propelling me here. Her face was fierce, determined. 'Hide,' she commanded. 'Hide.'

And so, I do. My pen is a torch cutting through the darkness. These pages are my lifeline, all I have to cling to.

I write to you, Anne, across the years, across the pain. You understand this fear. But more - you understand the power of words. How they bear witness. How they create light.

I write to carry on that light. To speak the truth in a time of lies. To keep hope alive, even as it slips away..."

The words pour out, a balm for my soul. My hand steadies as I write. I feel you with me, Anne. Together, we will endure."

My hand trembles as I put pen to paper once more.

The dim light in this cramped hiding spot strains my eyes, but I must write. It is the only thing keeping the panic at bay.

"I'm trapped in here Anne, unable to leave or help anyone. All I can do is bear witness to the horrors I've glimpsed outside. The gunfire and explosions have been relentless for hours. I hear screams, shouts, and the sound of running footsteps. My heart races, imagining who could be out there. Are my friends still alive? My family?

Writing to you, Anne, helps me feel less alone. But the truth is, I've never felt more isolated. Cut off from everyone and everything I know and love. I don't know how long I can last in this room. The walls seem to be closing in already.

My mind spins with questions. How much longer will this siege last? Will I run out of food and water? Should I risk trying to escape? I want to help, but my mother's last words echo in my mind: 'Hide. Hide.'

So, I write. I try to put my jumbled thoughts into words. If I can just get them on paper, maybe I'll feel less overwhelmed. Less powerless. This diary is the only control I have left. My chance to tell the story, no matter how it ends.

Anne, please stay with me. Lend me your courage to face the unknown. Help me hold on to hope, even now. I will keep writing, as long as I'm able. For you, for me, and for the truth."

My hand trembles as I grip the pen, but I force myself to keep writing. The scratch of the nib on the paper steadies me and gives me purpose. I pause, listening again to the sounds of warfare outside.

"Dear Anne,

The gunfire seems more distant now. Perhaps they have moved on to attack another part of the kibbutz. But for how long?

I think of my classmates and my teachers. Are they huddled in rooms like this one? Writing their own diaries? I imagine Rivka's bubbly laughter and Isaac's shy smile. Will I ever see them again? Hear their voices? Not knowing is almost worse than the fear.

At least in here, I have your words, Anne. Your diary gives me hope, even now. You faced such darkness with courage, finding light through writing. I will try to do the same. To be brave, though my whole body shakes.

Writing helps me remember who I am, beneath the fear. A girl who loves to read – who dreams of being a writer one day. I want to capture moments of beauty – like sunset over the wheat fields, and the smell of challah baking on Fridays. If I can hold those memories in my words, the violence outside cannot erase them.

I do not know what tomorrow will bring. But today, I will keep writing. One word at a

time, one story at a time. My words are a
flickering candle, pushing back the shadows,
helping me cling to faith. With you by my
side, Anne, I will find the strength to go on."

My hand slow, fingers cramping from gripping the pen so
tightly. I flex them, taking a deep breath before continuing.

"I'm so tired, Anne. Bone tired. This waiting,
not knowing - it's exhausting. I wish I could
sleep, and escape for just a little while. But
my dreams are filled with screams now,
seeing the same horrors over and over. Waking
is almost a relief, though the fear remains.

I envy your courage, your hope. Even when
you were stuck in the annex for years, you
found joy - in writing, in your family. The
world outside was falling apart, yet you held
on to optimism. I cling to that now,
imagining us as friends. You would tell me to
keep my chin up, to have faith.

So, I will try. For you, and for myself. Each word written is a small victory. My diary is a light cutting through the darkness. As long as I hold a pen, I have a purpose.

Stay with me, Anne. Help me find the strength to face another day. I will write to you again tomorrow, and all the tomorrows after. My words will keep us both alive."

I close the diary, pressing it to my heart. I feel lighter now, the swirling vortex of fear momentarily stilled. Writing has become my lifeline, connecting past and present. Anne's spirit will guide me through the days ahead. I tuck the diary back into its hiding spot, ready to face the uncertainty armed with the power of her words.

I creep back into the dusty corner, huddling against the cold concrete wall. I pull my knees to my chest, straining to hear any sounds from the world outside. But there is only silence - heavy and oppressive in this small, dark space.

I think of my mother, Leah. Is she still out there somewhere, hiding like I am? Or have the rockets found her, their explosions so loud they shatter windows for miles?

I squeeze my eyes shut, trying to block out the images. But they come anyway - fire, rubble, my mother's broken body lying lifeless on the ground.

A small sob escapes my lips before I can stop it. I quickly clamp my hand over my mouth. Any noise could give away my location if the wrong people are nearby.

I focus on my breathing, slow and steady, the way my father has taught me. In and out. Don't panic. He had always been my rock, solid and reassuring. Was he still that pillar of strength now? Or had the violence outside reduced him to a shell of the man he was?

I long to see them both again. To feel my mother's arms around me, and my father's big hand ruffling my hair. Are they out there right now, trying to find me? Or have they been forced to flee in the opposite direction when the sirens scream danger?

I shiver, the cold from the concrete seeping through my threadbare clothes. I think of my diary, tucked away safely. My one link to Anne Frank, to hope. I will write again soon. The words will keep me sane; it is the only thing that helps me to make sense of this nightmare.

For now, I wait in the darkness. Each moment of silence passing - another moment of survival. I must believe that somehow, someday, the light will return.

CHAPTER IV

I have made a friend in this isolation. My mind tries to convince me she is not real but, in my heart, I know she must be for me to survive. I have begun slowly taking myself to other places in my imagination. Miriam is my refuge. Reality and delusion have somehow found a way to merge that helps me make it through my day. Am I going insane? I think maybe so.

The ticking of the clock fills the silence of my room. I glance at the second hand, watching it march steadily onward. Another sleepless night ahead.

I shift restlessly beneath the blankets, thoughts swirling. The muted rumble of a jet passes overhead, its droning engines magnified in the stillness. I imagine the gleaming underbelly gliding through the inky night sky. Going somewhere. Anywhere but here.

A gentle knock at the door stirs me. I sit up, smoothing the covers.

"Come in," I call softly.

The door creaks open. Miriam's kind eyes find mine in the darkness. She steps inside, moving slowly to my bedside.

"Trouble sleeping again, my dear?"

I nod, dropping my gaze. Her weathered hand covers mine.

"I know, child. My mind plays the same tricks at night."

"I just want it to stop," I whisper.

Miriam squeezes my hand. "I cannot make it stop. But I can sit with you for a while."

She settles on the edge of the bed. The springs groan under her weight.

I lean into her, breathing in the faint scent of rosewater on her clothes. Her arm encircles my shoulders.

"Try to rest, Rachel. Morning always comes."

I close my eyes, focusing on the rise and fall of her chest. The rhythmic motion lulls me. For now, I am not alone.

This is a dream. It is not real, but my reality is far less believable, so I allow my imagination to take hold.

Miriam's soothing presence calms my racing thoughts. I cling to her, this lifeline in the darkness.

"Tell me again about the war," I murmur.

Miriam sighs, a faraway look in her eyes. "You know that story well, child."

"Please. It helps me understand."

She nods slowly, gathering the memories.

"It was long ago. I was just a girl, not much older than you."

I settle in, picturing a young Miriam weathering unimaginable storms.

"We took shelter night after night as bombs fell around us. Huddled together, praying for daylight."

I shudder, imagining the terror.

"There were times I thought the sun might never rise again. But it always did."

Her voice takes on a rhythmic cadence like she's spun this tale a hundred times before.

"We survived on rations and hope. Learned to find joy in the smallest of things - a long-hoarded chocolate bar, a letter from a loved one. Light piercing the rubble after an air raid."

I cling to every word, rapt. What I wouldn't give for such slivers of light in this darkness.

"It changed me, that war," Miriam continues. "Showed me how fragile yet resilient life can be."

She lifts my chin, meeting my anxious eyes.

"You have that same resilience, Rachel. This too shall pass."

I manage a small smile. With Miriam here, I can almost believe it.

I take a deep breath, steadying myself.

"I'm scared, Miriam. All the time. My heart races at every siren, every boom in the distance."

My voice quavers. She squeezes my hand.

"I know, child. But you cannot let the fear consume you. It will pass, as all things do."

Her calm certainty anchors me amidst the swirling chaos.

"How do you stay so strong?"

Miriam gazes out the window, thoughtfully.

"I have known darker times. But also, times of joy. You must look back at both, and know this moment is but a breath between them."

I try to envision it - life stretching before and behind, sorrow and laughter woven together.

"The light always returns," Miriam continues. "You must tend the flame inside you until it does."

The image ignites something within me. A spark of hope flickering in my heart.

"Is that what got you through the war?"

"Partly. We relied on the community too - knowing we survived together."

I think of my family and my friends. No matter what comes, we have each other.

"Thank you, Miriam." I squeeze her hand. "For reminding me there's still light ahead."

She smiles, eyes crinkling.

"You give me light too, child."

We sit in tranquil silence as dusk falls. The stillness comforts me.

Maybe the darkness won't last forever.

I take a deep breath as I open my diary. Writing has always been an escape for me, especially now.

Miriam's words echo in my mind. 'Look back at both sorrow and joy'. 'Tend the flame inside'.

I think back to our conversations, and the wisdom she's shared. She speaks of her own past - fleeing violence and losing loved ones. Yet still, she has hope.

I envy her resilience. When sirens blare, I cower in fear. But Miriam stands calmly, whispering "This too shall pass."

In her eyes, I see warmth amidst the weariness. She squeezes my hand, reminding me I have strength within me.

"You've endured so much already, child. This is but another test."

Her steadfast spirit lifts me up. She reminds me I'm not alone. We have a community, family.

Together, we'll weather this storm. Her experience is a light guiding us forward.

"Have faith," she says. "The dawn will come again."

I cling to her words now in the darkness. My pen flows, my spirit rising with each line.

Miriam's resilience runs through me. Her hope has kindled my own small flame.

As long as we nourish each other, it will burn bright.

I take a deep breath and continue writing in my diary. The dim candlelight flickers, casting dancing shadows across the walls of my room.

My mind drifts back to Miriam. She's now like a grandmother to me. I cherish our afternoon chats over tea, her wise words resonating deep within me.

There's a profound understanding between us - an unspoken bond forged through shared experience. She sees my inner light that I cannot always see myself.

When I cry out in despair, Miriam takes my hands in hers. Her skin is thin, etched with lines that tell of a long life's journey.

"You have already endured so much, my child," she says softly. "This burden may feel too heavy to bear, but your shoulders are stronger than you know."

I search for her kind eyes and see glimmers of her own hard-won strength. Miriam has known such darkness, yet still nurtures hope's tender flame.

She speaks of finding meaning amidst the rubble, of rebuilding even after the storm has passed. Miriam's resilience flows as deep and steady as an ancient river.

I confess my fear that I do not have her courage. She squeezes my hands tighter.

"Nonsense. You have everything you need inside you already. Write my dear, just write."

With Miriam as my guide, perhaps one day I will believe her words to be true. For now, I cling to them, taking one step at a time through the long night.

Some part of me knows my Miriam must be an Angel. For a brief moment, I feel protected.

I awaken before dawn, my breath catching in my throat. The nightmare fades, but a lingering unease remains.

I take up my pen with shaky hands. The familiar scratch of pen on paper soothes my rattled nerves.

Writing is my refuge, a raft amidst the roiling sea. As long as I can fill these pages, I have a purpose. Miriam's wisdom lives on through my words.

I strain to hear her lilting voice, imagine her sitting across from me. She would speak of cultivating inner strength, even now. Today I can't seem to conjure her.

"Darkness is but the canvas on which we paint light," she might say.

I yearn to embrace her. To thank Miriam for nurturing the seeds of resilience within me. My sapling courage has taken root in the shelter of her branches.

Perhaps one day this long night will end. We will emerge, blinking, into the dawn of a new day. I cling to the hope that I will stand beside my dear friend to witness it.

Until then, I will put pen to paper. My angel's light shines through me.

I take a deep breath to steady my nerves.

The specter of war looms, casting its shadow over our lives. Fear and uncertainty are constant companions. Yet where there is darkness, Miriam reminds me, light persists.

Her words are a balm, soothing my anxiety. She speaks of survival, of enduring despite the long odds. Miriam has walked this path before, emerging battered but unbroken.

I think of her stories, told in hushed tones by candlelight. Tales of resilience in the face of unimaginable horrors, of defiant hope flowering amidst the rubble.

Miriam shares these memories not to frighten, but to fortify. To show me that the human spirit can weather any storm. That even in our darkest hour, we must nurture the tender shoots of compassion.

She speaks and I listen, her voice a lifeline pulling me back from the brink of despair. Miriam reminds me I do not stand alone, though at times it feels thus.

I am grateful beyond words for her wisdom and for the shelter of her experience. She is the winding roots anchoring me firmly in place as storms rage overhead.

I will weather this long night as she has weathered so many before. And in the quiet moments between the thunderclaps, I will write. Bearing witness, holding fast to hope, illuminating the darkness one word at a time.

Miriam's light shines on through me.

With a trembling hand, I lift my pen. The blank page awaits, hungry for words unspoken.

Where to begin? The shadows encroach as I search for a foothold. But then Miriam's face appears - her kind eyes crinkling with warmth, silver hair framing her careworn face. She nods, a silent prompt to continue.

I inhale, steadying my nerves. The pen touches the paper.

"My dear friend,"

I write - each letter a small victory over the looming dark.

"Even in this bleakest hour, you give me strength."

I describe Miriam's tranquility, her unshakable poise. How she moves through the world with grace, soothing those around her. The shelter of her small home, candles burning as we shared our stories.

The pen flows freely now. I write of hope, of light piercing the darkness. Of new beginnings stirring beneath the rubble. Of hands joined in defiance of hate.

These words I commit to paper, my own act of resistance. Though the night presses close, I will not surrender this small space of light.

With Miriam as my guide, I will nurture the seeds of a new dawn. And when the sun rises, healing and renewal will bloom. For she has walked this path before - she knows the darkness ends.

I conclude:

"Your light inspires me, Miriam. With you, I know I can endure."

Setting down the pen, I feel the weight of the long night begin to lift. The first pale rays of a new day glow at the horizon.

Hope lives on through these words. Miriam's light continues to shine.

CHAPTER V

My hands tremble as I clutch my diary, its blue leather binding creaking under my tight grip. I sink onto the thin mattress in the corner of the safe room, the concrete underneath, unforgiving. Taking a shaky breath, I try to calm my racing heart before it bursts from my chest.

With fumbling fingers, I open to a fresh, blank page. The paper glares up at me, impatient for the dance of ink that will soon grace its surface. I pause, listening. The distant thuds of mortar fire punctuate the heavy silence. Each explosion makes my breath catch; my palms grow slick with sweat. I strain my ears for any sign of planes overhead, rockets screaming through the sky. But for now, only silence.

I poise my pen over the paper, thoughts churning. How to capture the maelstrom inside? My longing for Mama, for Yael, not knowing if-- No. I squeeze my eyes shut, pushing the thoughts away. Survive each moment. One word at a time.

The pen touches the paper. I begin to write.

"Dear Anne,

The gunfire started before dawn today. I woke to pops and cracks that sounded closer than before. My heart raced as I huddled here on this mattress, clutching my blanket tight. I squeezed my eyes shut and tried to breathe, knowing it would pass. But the sounds went on and on.

I thought of Yael. Is she safe? Have her parents gotten her to a shelter too? I pray that cheerful grin of hers isn't dimmed by fear. That her bright spirit stays strong through all of this. Yael, I hope you know that I'm here, thinking of you. You're the sister of my heart and soul. Please be okay.

And Mama and Papa. Are you together, wherever you are? Staying strong for each other as you always have? I know you're thinking of me just as much as I'm thinking of you now. I hope these walls and distance between us can't stop our love from reaching across. I feel you here with me, even in the darkest moments. We'll be together again soon. This can't last forever.

But for now, I wait. And hope. And write. One word at a time, one page after another. My thoughts flow through this pen, taking shape on these pages. This diary anchors me when fear threatens to pull me adrift. Within these covers, I find my strength."

I pause, blinking back the sting in my eyes as I gently blow on the ink to dry it. The gunfire has faded for now. But I know it's only a matter of time before it starts again. Until then, I have these pages. And hope.

I take a shaky breath, staring down at the page. The words blur before my eyes as tears well up. I blink them back, gripping my pen tighter.

"I can't stop thinking about you today. Trapped in that tiny secret annex for years, never knowing if each day would be your last. Surrounded by death and darkness, but still

I pause, a lump in my throat as I picture the slight, dark-haired girl who has become like a sister to me through her words.

I gently trace my fingers over Anne's name, taking a deep, shaky breath as I feel her presence like a whisper in my heart. I'm not alone. Anne's spirit is here, lighting my way through the dark.

I close my eyes, picturing in my mind the world I dream of. A world at peace. I see children playing outside, their laughter ringing through the streets. I see families gathered around dinner tables, chatting and smiling, no longer afraid. I see people of all religions and backgrounds coming together, embracing their differences instead of fighting.

I imagine the skies cleared of smoke; the streets free of rubble. No more wailing sirens or booming explosions to make me jump. No more nights spent curled up in this basement room, my stomach gnawing with hunger. Just light and laughter and hope.

Opening my eyes, I sigh deeply, clutching my diary tighter. The sounds of war still rumble outside, but I must keep visualizing that peaceful world. I must keep writing, and keep dreaming, even when everything seems dark.

Anne showed me how light can exist even in the darkest corners. How one voice whispering hope is louder than a thousand bombs. I may be just a girl, but my words have power. My dreams and resilience can be a torch to guide others through fear and despair.

I am not helpless. I am strong. I will keep writing. I will keep hoping. I will survive this and one day, somehow, help make my dream of peace come true.

The muffled crump of explosions shakes the walls, but I try to shut it out. I take a deep breath and turn to a fresh page in my diary.

"Miriam's kind face floats into my mind. My imagined elderly neighbor checks on me every day, bringing scraps of food and a reassuring pat on the hand. Her silver hair reminds me of moonbeams, and her eyes are twin pools of wisdom. She has lived through so much, yet still nurtures hope.

'We have survived worse, little one,' she tells me, squeezing my hand.

'There is light ahead, even if we cannot yet see it.'

I cling to her words through the long hours in this safe room. Miriam knows the darkness intimately, but she does not surrender to it. Her quiet strength gives me courage when I feel I have none.

When the bombs fell too close yesterday, when I shook with panic, Miriam held me tight. 'Breathe with me,' she whispered. 'We will get through this.'"

My pen pauses, listening. Faintly, from the rubble outside, birdsong lifts into the air. Notes of fragile hope. Life is still clinging amidst the wreckage.

I close my eyes, letting those sweet notes seep into my heart. If the birds still sing, there is reason to believe. Light peeking through clouds.

I am not alone. Miriam's love surrounds me. The birds remind me that even in the darkest times, hope takes flight on fragile wings. If I hold onto these glimmers, I will make it through the night.

I reopen my diary with trembling hands, the pages crinkled from being clutched so often. The leather cover is worn smooth, imprinted with my anxieties. Each day I pour my heart into these pages. My diary has become a faithful friend, absorbing my fears so they do not consume me. Is that how it felt for you, my dearest Anne?

The pen feels heavy today. I pause, listening to my own shaky breathing, trying to find the words. The chaos outside continues unabated. I want to block my ears, to hide from it all.

Instead, I begin to write. The pen scratches softly, etching my innermost thoughts. I describe the exact shade of darkness, the smell of dust and smoke. The pen does not flinch from the truth.

Slowly, my breathing steadies. The blank page clears my mind and makes space for whatever needs to emerge. The diary bears witness without judgment. I confess my terror, my longing for normalcy, my bone-deep exhaustion.

Catharsis comes in naming the demons. I peel back the layers of fear, exposing my raw and aching heart. The pen is merciful, letting me give shape to formless dread.

When the words finally stop flowing, I feel cleansed. Lighter. The diary has drawn poison from my soul. It is a light in the darkness, a place where my spirit can take refuge. No matter how broken the world becomes, this book will hold me together. I whisper thanks to the silent pages, filled with gratitude for their solace. My diary, my truest friend in chaos. My Anne.

CHAPTER VI

The sudden boom of the explosion shakes the walls around me. My heart drops into my stomach as the ground trembles beneath my feet. The roar lingers, echoing against the concrete walls. I press my hands over my ears, trying to block out the deafening sound.

My breath comes in ragged gasps as the dust settles. The air is choked with smoke and the acrid smell of explosives. I feel my panic rising as the ringing in my ears subsides. The barrage of gunfire and rockets outside continues, a constant reminder of the danger that surrounds me.

I'm paralyzed, frozen in place. My eyes dart around the small safe room, taking in the bare walls and piles of supplies. This cramped space is all that separates me from the chaos outside. I feel so small and helpless, like a scared little mouse hiding in its hole.

My hands tremble as I clutch my diary to my chest. The worn cover and frayed pages are familiar and comforting. Opening it calms my racing heart, even just a little. I flip through the entries, some, my words, some Anne's. Her courage gives me strength and helps me push past the fear. If she could find hope amid such darkness, maybe I can too.

I take a shaky breath and poise my pen over the blank page. The words pour out of me, an outlet for my jumbled thoughts. I write about the explosion, the acrid smoke, the uncertainty gnawing at my core. The pen scratches steadily, grounding me. If I can put these emotions into words, I know I'll survive whatever comes next. Anne's spirit is with me, her diary a light cutting through the darkness.

The pounding of my heart drowns out the chaos outside. I'm numb, struggling to process the nightmare unfolding around me.

My fingers tighten around the edges of Anne's diary, the worn cover is soft and familiar in my hands. It's my lifeline, my sanctuary. With shaky hands, I open it, comforted by the sight of Anne's elegant script alongside my own messy scrawl.

Seeing our words side by side steadies me, even just a little. Anne gives me courage and helps me push past the paralyzing fear. I take a deep breath and put pen to paper.

The pen continues scratching, my diary a refuge amidst the chaos. Anne's light shines on, guiding me forward one written word at a time.

The explosion rocks the walls, the force of it nearly knocks me off the mattress. My heart hammers against my ribs as dust rains down from the ceiling. This is too close.

I press the pen harder to the page, my hand shaking. I will write about the deafening boom, and the way it vibrated through my bones. The not-knowing where or how bad tears me apart inside.

My thoughts go to Mama and Papa again. Are they okay? Did they make it to the shelter in time? And Yael - is her family safe? I pray they found cover. I can't lose them.

The pen digs into the page as I scribble faster. Getting the words out is my lifeline, the only control I have in this chaos. I tell Anne how scared I am, how I wish I could be brave like her. She gives me strength even now.

The sounds of gunfire and sirens pierce the air. I want to cover my ears, to block it all out. But I will keep writing. I tell Anne I'm trying to hold onto hope, but it's getting harder. My hand aches as I spill my heart onto the page.

When I finally lift my pen, I feel drained but steady. Anne's spirit is with me, her diary a light cutting through the darkness. I close my eyes, summoning every bit of courage. If she can face her fate with grace, so can I.

I take a deep, shuddering breath as I close my diary. The pen falls from my limp fingers. My racing heart begins to slow as I cling to the familiar weight of the book in my hands. Anne's words echo in my mind —

"I still believe, in spite of everything, that people are truly good at heart." (Frank, 1991)

I want to believe that too. But the constant sounds of sirens and explosions make it hard. I feel so small and powerless, locked away while the world falls apart outside these walls.

My leg bounces with nervous energy. I wish I could pace,
but the safe room is tiny. I'm trapped, just like Anne was.
But she never lost hope. She found light even in the darkness
of the annex. I envy her courage.

The air feels thick and heavy, like a weight pressing down
on my chest. I struggle to take full breaths. Writing helps -
it gives me purpose. The words flowing from my pen keep
me tethered, stopping me from spiraling into panic.

I know Mama and Papa would tell me to have faith. To
pray, and trust that we'll make it through this. I close my
eyes, imagining their faces. If we stay strong, we can
survive, just like Anne did for so long. Her spirit gives me
the strength I need to face whatever comes next.

I grip my pen tighter, the familiar shape a comfort in my
hand. The explosions outside are getting louder. I imagine
the chaos beyond these walls - homes destroyed, people
fleeing for their lives. My heart races and I take a shaky
breath, trying to stay calm.

The pen moves across the page almost of its own accord.
The words tumble out in a jumbled rush, an outlet for my
fear and anxiety. I write about the helplessness I feel, locked

away while danger looms. How I wish I could be brave, like Anne. She faced each day in the annex with a quiet courage I can't comprehend.

The diary anchors me, giving me a sense of purpose amidst the uncertainty. If I keep writing, I have some control. Some way to make sense of things, even if only on paper. I think of Anne's words again —

"I want to go on living even after my death." (Frank, 1991)

Her voice, preserved in ink, resonates through the years.

My words may not have the same impact, but they matter to me. Each sentence is proof that I endured this. That I didn't give up hope, even when it seemed foolish to hope at all. I will fill these pages, taking strength from Anne's spirit within me. Her legacy reminds me - if I can write, I can survive.

I clutch the diary tightly, my knuckles white. The pen shakes in my grip as I press it to the page once more.

"Dear Anne,

My thoughts turn to Yael. Her bright laughter echoes in my memory. I picture her fiery curls, always escaping her braids. Her freckled nose crinkles as she tells a joke. Is she safe? Has she found shelter too? I ache not knowing, feeling her absence like a missing limb.

We'd planned to see a movie next weekend. Something frivolous and fun, to forget our troubles for a while. I wonder if we'll ever get the chance. If I'll ever again link my arm through hers as we walk down the street. Not knowing is a constant knot in my stomach."

I pour these worries into my diary.

"Anne, wherever you are, please watch over Yael too. Keep her safe. My words can't shield her, but maybe my faith can. I must believe we'll laugh together again one day. For now,

I let out a long breath as I closed the diary, the tense set of my shoulders softening. For a moment, the constant rumble of explosions and gunfire fade into the background. Holding my diary grounds me, its solid weight and smooth cover soothing.

Running my fingers over the embossed letters of my name, I'm reminded of why I write. Someday, I hope my words can make a difference. That people in the future will read my story, just as I read Anne's. They'll know what it was like to huddle in fear as the world crashed down around us.

Maybe my words will inspire them, just as Anne's inspired me. Remind them not to lose hope, even in humanity's darkest hours. As long as we keep writing, and keep sharing our truth, we have a light to guide us.

Closing my eyes, I hug the diary to my chest. The sounds of war rumble menacingly, but I push down my fear. I am not alone. Anne's spirit is with me, and the spirits of all those who write to be heard. Their strength flows through my pen, and if I keep writing, I can survive anything.

I open my eyes and take a deep breath, steeling myself. The air in the safe room is stale and suffocating. How long have I been here? Hours? Days? Weeks? Time blurs together.

My hands tremble, but I clutch the diary tighter. The solidity of it comforts me. If I have my words, I am not alone.

Anne's voice echoes in my mind:

"I still believe, in spite of everything, that people are truly good at heart." (Frank, 1991)

I want to believe that too, but it's so hard. Each explosion makes me flinch, wondering if a rocket has hit our building. Have we been found? Are they coming for us?

I strain my ears, heart pounding. All I hear is muffled chaos. The walls protect me, but they feel like a prison. I'm cut off, isolated. Are my parents still alive out there? My friends?

I long to see sunlight again, to feel fresh air. To know that we've survived this nightmare. But all I can do is wait in this cold, dark box. Write and pray we will make it through.

My pen trembles, but I start a new diary entry. The words pour out in a rush. I write about my fear, my hopes, and everything I dare not speak aloud. The pages soak up my emotions like a sponge.

With each word, I feel a bit stronger. This diary tethers me to hope. If I write, I have a reason to endure. My story will live on, even if I don't.

I may be trapped here, but my words can fly free.

CHAPTER VII

I open my diary, the crisp pages crackling beneath my trembling fingers.

"Dear Anne,"

I write, though my hero feels impossibly far away.

"Yael. Her name drifts through my mind, carrying on the echoes of our laughter. I see her fiery curls bouncing as we run through the streets, hand-in-hand, breathless and free. Now the streets are filled with soldiers, their boots pounding out a sinister beat.

Where are you, Yael? Have you found a hiding place? Are you safe? My heart aches not knowing. I wish I could see your smile again and be wrapped in one of your fierce hugs. The world is so much darker without you in it.

This room feels cavernous, the silence heavy. I long to hear your voice, rich with mischief and life. Our secrets, once whispered eagerly back and forth, now rattle unspoken inside me.

Oh, Yael. My dearest friend. Come back to me."

The stillness presses down, suffocating. I strain to hear any stirrings, any signs of life beyond these walls. Nothing. Only the pounding of blood in my ears, the raspy shudder of each breath.

My fingers tremble, struggling to form the letters.

"I have to believe you're out there, Yael. That we'll laugh together again one day."

Even as I write the words, doubt creeps in. Are such hopes foolish? Naive?

"I recall our escape, the panic rising in your eyes as we fled. My last glimpse of your beloved face before the hidden door closed between us. I cling to that image now. Let it be seared into my memory, not replaced by anything darker.

Each minute without you is an eternity. Time moves differently in this limbo between life and death. I mark its passing by the changing light through the cracks between my door and frame. Dawn comes. Dusk falls. Day after day after day.

But I cannot give up. I will keep writing, keep waiting, keep hoping. For you, my dear Yael. Until we meet again."

The light fades, plunging me into shadow. I fumble for the candle, hands shaking as I light the wick. A small, flickering glow pierces the darkness.

Shadows dance across the bare walls. This tiny room is both a haven and a prison. I long to see the moon again and feel the wind on my face. Simple freedoms are now luxuries beyond reach.

"Yael, how I wish you were here. You lit up every room with your vibrant spirit. Your optimism was contagious, even in the bleakest times. Without you, loneliness threatens to swallow me whole.

I picture your face, etched with laughter, eyes shining. The memories bring me comfort, but also sorrow. Are we still the same carefree girls who whispered and giggled late into the night? Or has this war carved away that innocence, leaving hardened shells behind?

Perhaps we must change to survive. But I hope we can still find slivers of light, even here. That we can keep trusting, keep hoping, and keep loving.

Let this be my silent promise, Yael – I will hold onto the goodness in me, the goodness in you. However long it takes, I will wait for our reunion. A single candle can illuminate the dark. Your memory is the flame that sustains me."

I set down the pen, flexing my cramped fingers. The sound of my pen on paper is my only companion now. I pour my innermost thoughts onto these pages, baring my soul to an unseen audience.

"Anne, do you hear my whispers in the night? I cling to the image of you, huddled over your own diary, finding solace in writing as I do. Perhaps we are not so different, two girls isolated from the world, seeking meaning amidst the chaos."

My mind turns to a boy I have seen in the kibbutz: Eitan.

"Dear Anne,

There is a boy named Eitan, much like your Peter. I don't know him well, only glimpses from afar. I imagine him moving through the shadows, speaking little, helping others. Kindness glimmers in those sea-green eyes. He wouldn't hesitate to share what little he has.

I imagine what he would say if we were hidden here together. Would he tell me stories to pass the time? Sing songs in his deep, gentle voice? Or would we sit in easy silence, speaking without words?

I feel less alone picturing him nearby. His inner light would complement my darkness, creating a beautiful balance. In my dreams, he takes my hand, a reassuring anchor in the storm.

Wakefulness always shatters the illusion. But the memory of his face sustains me, as does yours, Anne. If I can write, I won't lose myself entirely. My words are breadcrumbs leading back to hope."

Yours,

Rachel"

The sound of my writing fills the quiet. I pause, listening for hints of danger, but hear only my shallow breathing.

"Anne, I wish I could speak to you beyond these pages. To hear your voice, rich with life and spirit despite all you've endured. We both know the pain of losing friends, watching our worlds unravel thread by thread.

But Eitan gives me hope. In him, I see strength emerging from adversity. He never stops fighting for those in need, even at great risk. I think of when Hamas came, dragging Mr. Abramowitz into the street. Eitan ran forward, pleading for mercy until they struck him down. He rose slowly, blood dripping from his lip, but did not retreat. I fear that is the last time I will ever see him.

I ache to know him, to unravel the mystery that shrouds this boy. What memories haunt those sea-green eyes? What dreams fill his restless sleep? In unguarded moments, I catch glimpses of his longing for connection. If only I could reach through the distance between us.

My imaginings are a salve, but no substitute for his real presence. I cling to the belief that we aren't always alone, even when it feels that way. Someday, the shadows will lift. Until then, I'll keep writing, breathing life into my silent hopes. Anne, stay with me."

I pause, listening for footsteps outside my door. Hearing nothing, I continue writing:

"The air is heavy tonight, weighed down by fear and uncertainty. I can't sleep, thoughts racing like panicked heartbeats.

If only I could speak to Eitan. He would know what to say to steady me. I imagine his voice, soft but strong. 'Rachel, breathe with me. We'll get through this together.' I sync my breaths with the rise and fall of his chest, feeling calmer.

He tells me of his little sister, Sarah, whose giggles once filled their home. She saw beauty everywhere, even in broken things. He vows to protect that light in her memory.

I confess my own fears – of being forgotten, losing those I love. He squeezes my hand gently. 'I will remember you, Rachel. No one can take that away.'

I know these conversations exist only in my longing. But I'm grateful for a companion, imaginary yet real to me. For a moment, I don't feel so alone.

Anne, did you have someone who comforted you in the dark? I hope you did. And that with Peter you found the connection you dreamed of. For now, I'll keep writing, giving shape to the hope that I can find this as well."

I nod off, pen still in hand. A loud bang jolts me awake. Muffled shouts filter through the walls. I hold my breath, straining to make out the words. Are they searching for me? Have they found my hiding spot?

My heart pounds as I creep to the door and peer out. All is silent once more. Just my imagination playing tricks, I tell myself. I slide down against the wall, hugging my knees to my chest.

Get it together, Rachel. Focus on what you can control. I open my diary again, the familiar action steadying me. My pen moves slowly, writing each letter with care.

"Dear Anne,

Today I vow to be brave. To cling to hope when fear closes in. To search for light even in the darkest of days. I will write and remember every word, every face, every moment that matters. If I don't survive, maybe these pages will. Maybe someone will find them one day and know - we were here. We lived, we loved, we tried to make it through the night.

This diary connects me to you, Anne, and all who came before. When your words endure, you live on. I hope mine will too. This is my legacy, my candle in the window, shining through the darkness.

Love,

I sign my name with a flourish, a small act of defiance. They can take everything else, but they can't take my voice. As long as I can write, I have a purpose. I am still Rachel. This has become my mantra.

CHAPTER VIII

More muffled booms shake the walls. I press my back against the cold concrete, eyes darting around the cramped space. This so-called "safe" room is barely larger than a closet. Nothing about this feels safe.

My heart pounds with each explosion, sounding closer than the last. I want to cover my ears but can't lift my trembling hands. Will the next blast break through the door? The uncertainty gnaws at me.

I imagine the destruction outside. Buildings in ruins, fires raging, people screaming. Images from news footage and movies flash through my mind in an endless loop. Is this our new reality?

My thoughts drift back to Anne Frank, hidden away for years in an attic not much bigger than this. At least she had her family. I'm alone, not knowing if mine are alive or dead. Not knowing is the worst, feeding the dark scenarios my anxious mind conjures.

I long for the simple comforts - a soft bed, my favorite sweater, and a cup of hot tea. Things I took for granted not long ago before the siege on our city began. Now they seem lifetimes away.

Gunfire cracks, bringing me back. I yearn for silence, stillness, safety. But all I feel is the cold floor beneath me. I hear the sounds of war drawing nearer. I cling to the hope that each explosion will be the last. I pray that soon there will be quiet, and I will step outside to find the people I love, unharmed.

Until then, I will stay here and write. My pen stills my trembling hand, as I etch the memories of our lives before. Of happier days I pray we'll know again.

The pounding in my chest grows louder than the bombardment outside. I close my eyes, trying to slow my ragged breaths, to regain some small measure of calm.

But the images continue flashing, each more terrifying than the last. Bodies littering the streets, homes collapsed to rubble, flames engulfing everything we know. Are those visions or realities? I don't know anymore.

I want to block it out, all of it. The sights and sounds envelop me, the dark thoughts overwhelm me. I want to be somewhere else, anywhere else.

Maybe I can escape by writing. Lose myself in memories of the life I took for granted only recently. My family gathered around the dinner table, laughing over silly stories. My best friend and I, daydreaming about our future travels. Simple moments I realize now were everything.

The pen trembles in my hand as I etch those memories. I cling to them, even as the walls shake and gunfire rages on. They ground me, reminding me there are still good things in this world worth fighting for. Worth surviving for.

So, I keep writing, bearing witness to this day. Hoping beyond hope for the chance to write of better ones when this is finally over. My words feel so small against the destruction, but they are all I have that sustains me now.

I glance around the cramped space I now call home. Four cold walls, a tiny sliver of light from the doorway. It's a far cry from the warm rooms and laughter that filled our house.

Anne's attic, at least, had a window. She could look outside and see the chestnut tree and a sliver of sky. She had Peter and her family, people to talk to, share food with, and take comfort in. Here, it's just me and the demons in my mind.

The explosions sound closer now, the walls trembling with each blast. I wonder how long it will take until they find me here. If they will come, crashing through the door, guns blazing, my hiding spot exposed.

I wish I could speak to Anne and have her answer back. I would ask her how she stayed so hopeful, so resilient when death lurked right outside. Did she have days where she lost faith, where the waiting and isolation seemed unbearable? I bet she did. After all, she was just a girl too. Scared and longing for it to be over.

But she kept writing. Kept believing in the goodness of people, even when hatred surrounded her. I must believe that too. I must cling to the thought that one day, we'll emerge from this darkness into light. That fear and violence won't reign forever.

The explosions grow faint. Perhaps they've moved on. I breathe a cautious sigh of relief and keep writing. One word at a time, searching for meaning amidst the chaos. Moving toward that distant dawn, when peace will come again.

The silence unnerves me even more than the explosions. At least with the bombs, I knew they were out there. Now, anything could be happening beyond these walls.

Are people still fighting? Have they fled, searching for safety like me? Is the battle moving away, or are they regrouping, planning their next attack?

I strain my ears for any clue but only hear my own shaky breathing. I want to break free from this tomb and see it with my own eyes. Make sure my family has survived another day.

But I know I can't. The battlefield remains too unpredictable. One misstep could mean the end.

So, I wait, trapped in limbo. Seconds stretch into minutes, minutes into hours. Time loses meaning when each moment could be your last.

My fingers tremble as I grip the pen tighter.

"The urge to burst out of this cage builds inside me. I long to run to my family and find them huddled together, shaken, but alive.

Instead, I pour my restless energy into these pages. Write to feel connected to something beyond this purgatory. To leave a trace of myself behind, in case I don't make it through."

The waiting continues. I will keep writing.

"The walls feel like they're closing in on me. The stale air burns my throat with each breath. I yearn for a breeze, for the feeling of warm sand beneath my feet instead of cold concrete.

My stomach rumbles, but I barely notice. Hunger means nothing when death hovers so near. I'd trade a hundred meals for one more minute with the people I love. To see their faces, hear their voices. Make sure we haven't lost each other yet.

I strain my ears again, clinging to the hope that the battle has ended. But only silence greets me. No cries of victory or wails of defeat. Just this torturous nothingness.

I want to scream just to break the monotony. Pound my fists against the walls until they crumble, or my hands break. Anything to release this pent-up desperation.

But I stay frozen in place. Making noise could give away my location if the enemy lurks nearby. I must keep it together and stay alert. Surviving means keeping my fear bottled up inside.

The waiting continues. I focus on my breathing, in and out, willing my heart to slow down. I tell myself my family is safe, that we'll all make it through this. That one day, we'll sit around the dinner table again, whole and reunited.

For now, these pages are my only comfort. In them, I find order amidst the chaos. Proof that I'm still here, still holding on. That no matter what comes next, my voice has been heard."

I stare down at the diary resting in my lap, tracing my fingers over the worn cover. My name is etched into the leather, the letters faded but still legible.

I wonder if Anne felt as alone as I do now, isolated in her tiny room in the annex. At least she had the comfort of whispered conversations, muffled laughter, hushed arguments. Signs of life, persisting, even in hiding.

Here in this cramped shelter, all I have is the sound of my breathing and the pounding of blood in my ears. Each minute ticks by as if an eternity.

Still, Anne's words give me hope. She found light even in her darkest days. Her voice reached millions, decades after her own was silenced.

If she can inspire others through her diary, maybe I can too. These pages contain the truth of what happened here. One day, they could remind the world of the lives lost and the suffering endured.

I will write for all those who can't. The children huddled in basements, the mothers searching for their families, the old men buried in rubble. Someone must tell their stories.

Anne believed people were good at heart. I must believe it too, despite everything. That someday, we'll have peace again.

Until then, all I can do is keep writing. My pen is the only weapon I have left.

A deafening explosion shakes the walls. I drop my pen as dust rains down from the ceiling. This one sounded close. Too close.

I scramble to my feet, my heart hammering. How much longer can the room withstand this barrage? I press my ear to the cold metal door. Muffled shouts and cries filter through. The battle rages just outside.

My throat tightens. What if the soldiers break through? Will I be gunned down here, alone and afraid, like so many others?

No. I can't think like that. Fear is the real enemy here. If I give in, I've already lost.

I force myself to breathe, wiping dust from the diary pages. Anne made it two years in hiding. I can endure a little longer.

The sounds of warfare fade for a moment. In the stillness, I hear a soft whimper. A child's cry. It comes from the air vent near the ceiling.

Someone else has found shelter in this building. A small voice to remind me I'm not alone after all. We will weather this storm together.

I sit back down and pick up my pen, comforted. If we share our light, even the darkest night will end. The dawn will come again. I believe this with all my heart.

Until then, I will write and hope.

CHAPTER IX

Again, I clutch my diary to my chest, the edges digging into my skin. My heartbeat pounds in my ears as I sit curled in the corner of the safe room. The air is musty and stale, faint rays of light filtering in through the narrow slits between the concrete walls and the door.

I can't stop thinking about Eitan. His quiet strength and gentle smile fill my thoughts, even though I haven't seen him since I was rushed down here. I remember the way his green eyes crinkled at the edges when he laughed, his deep voice teasing me playfully. If things were different, we'd sit side-by-side, talking for hours. He would listen so intently like every word I said mattered.

I trace my fingers over the worn pages of my diary as I allow my imagination to wander and dream. Eitan and I walked hand-in-hand through the quiet streets, the moonlight casting everything in an ethereal glow. We don't need to speak - just being together is enough. I feel so safe with him. So understood.

The wail of distant sirens makes my heart clench. I squeeze my eyes shut, imagining Eitan's arms around me, his breath warm against my hair.

"It's going to be okay, Rachel," he would say.

And I would believe him. Because with Eitan, I would feel like I could survive anything, even this.

He gives me hope. A light in all this darkness. My fingers tremble as I grip the pen, writing a silent promise to him across the page.

"I will find you again one day. I must believe that."

The sirens fade, leaving only tense silence. I take a shaky breath, opening my eyes to the dim light of the shelter.

My thoughts drift back to Eitan. To his quiet strength and courage. He always protects those who need it, no matter the cost to himself.

I imagine a day when a group of boys corner Sammy, a boy from our school, in the alley behind the bakery. Sammy cowering against the bricks as they taunt him, ready to strike. But then Eitan appears, stepping between them.

"Walk away," he says, voice steady.

The boys just laugh. When one grabs Sammy's shirt, Eitan doesn't hesitate. He shoves the bully back hard. The others advance, but Eitan holds his ground, green eyes blazing.

"I said walk away," he repeats.

Something in his tone must have convinced them. The boys back off slowly, casting dirty looks over their shoulders as they leave.

Eitan turns to Sammy, gently helping him up. "Are you okay?" Sammy nods shakily. Eitan walks him home, making sure he gets there safely. He never tells anyone. But I see it all.

Even then, I know - Eitan is the type of person who runs toward danger to help others. Not away. My heart aches thinking of him out there now, being brave while I hide here, helpless.

I wish I could be strong like I imagine him to be. I wish I could fight back against the fear trying to consume me. But all I can do is wait in the dark, writing words that may never reach him, and hope we will meet again.

I close my eyes and picture his face - those piercing green eyes that seem to stare right through me. In my mind, I traced the line of his jaw. I imagine reaching out to brush back that unruly lock of hair that's always falling across his forehead.

Our time together replays like scenes from a movie. I see us sitting under the old oak tree behind the school, sunlight dappling the grass. We speak very little out loud, but a whole conversation flows silently between us. In the quiet, I feel the calmest I've ever been.

In my mind, I picture a day at the market when gunfire erupts nearby. Shoppers panic, fleeing every which way. But Eitan grips my hand tightly, leading me swiftly to safety in a storefront. And though my heart races with fear, his steady presence keeps me grounded.

During these precious moments we share, an unspoken bond is forged. In Eitan, I find someone who understands this life we've been handed. Someone facing the same darkness, but still fighting to see the light.

Now I ache for the reassurance of his hand in mine. My soul calls out for the shelter of his arms. I want to unburden all these knotted fears and have him soothe them with his quiet wisdom.

My dear Eitan, how I wish we could weather this storm side by side, drawing courage from one another. Though we're apart, know that you remain in my heart always. Stay strong and come back to me safely. The light of our future together will guide me through the nights ahead.

I close my eyes and picture our reunion. The air raid sirens finally quiet, the all-clear sounds. I emerge from the shelter into the hazy morning light. And there you are, beloved Eitan, weary and worn but still standing strong.

I run to you and feel your arms enfold me. The relief brings tears that dampen your shoulder, as you smooth my hair and murmur soothing words. In this moment, nothing else matters but being here with you.

We walk hand in hand through the rubble-strewn streets in contemplative silence. There is so much to take in, so much lost and changed forever. What will become of our city, our people, you and me? The future once seemed vast with possibility, now it looms uncertain.

But with you by my side, I feel a flicker of hope. If we can weather this darkest hour together, perhaps we can build a new life from the ashes. Though the path ahead won't be easy, I know our bond will sustain us. Come what may in this broken world, I will walk into that unknown future with you, my love.

Our tender feelings will be forged in the crucible of war. Perhaps it's strange that my heart stirs for you amidst so much suffering and loss. But your strength and compassion shine bright even in these dark days. You are a beacon that guides me through the long fearful nights.

I picture our last moment together before the terror strikes begin. We walk hand in hand through the quiet evening streets, the setting sun casting everything in a golden glow. You pick a flower from someone's garden and tuck it behind my ear, your fingers lingering softly on my cheek. We exchange smiles filled with shy promises.

Just then, the sirens begin to wail, shattering the stillness. We ran towards the shelter, the flower falling forgotten to the ground. I recall the panic in your eyes mirroring my own, your hand gripping mine tightly as we fled. We didn't know it would be our last moment of peace for so long. I'm not sure how long I had been running before I realized my hand was no longer in yours. I'm not sure where you are or what happened. All I can do is hope for the best and pray that you are okay.

Now as I sit alone writing by candlelight, I cling to the memories of you that sustain me. I think of your kindness, your strength, your bright spirit undimmed by the surrounding darkness. My heart swells with emotion I cannot yet fully grasp.

Perhaps these feelings are born of proximity and need. But they feel so real, a shining light in my darkest hour. I long for the day I will see your beloved face again. Until then, I hold you in my heart, a cherished flame of hope that cannot be extinguished.

I stare at the blank pages before me, grasping for the right words to convey everything I feel. It no longer matters if things are real or imagined. It is a different world in my little personal prison and no rules apply. My hand trembles as I lift the pen, imaginary emotions spilling forth.

"My dearest Eitan,

In these last fraught days, you have been a steady anchor when everything else felt adrift. Your calm voice in my mind soothes my restless spirit. The memory of your warm gaze gives me courage when fear creeps close. Even in silence, you impart strength.

I confess I hardly knew you before the sirens wailed, yet now I cannot imagine my life without you nearby. This may seem strange, for we are little more than strangers. But in the crucible of war, bonds are forged quickly and true.

You saw me - really saw me - behind the fear. And you made me feel I could be brave, even when bravery eluded me. For that, and for every quiet act of kindness, I am forever grateful.

The future is obscured, the present fraught with sorrow. But I will hold hope close, stoking its embers until the day we meet again. Stay safe, my friend. Know you are in my every thought and prayer. If we make it through this darkness, I believe a bright new dawn awaits us both. Until then, all my love across the distance.

Yours always,

Rachel"

I carefully blot the ink before closing my diary. Sleep will not come easy tonight, but writing has settled my restless mind. I cling to the hope of seeing Eitan again as I blow out the candle and wait for dawn's first light. Whatever comes, I will face it with his memory engraved on my heart.

CHAPTER X

My heart pounds against my chest as I huddle in the corner of the safe room. The air is musty and still, muted sounds filtering through the walls - footsteps pacing, muffled voices. I strain to make out the words, but they are too distorted. Who is out there? What are they planning?

Each creak of the floorboards and each shuffle of feet makes my breath catch in my throat. I want to melt into the walls and disappear completely. Maybe then I'll be safe. But I know that's just a fantasy, a vain hope. All I can do is wait here in the crushing darkness, my imagination conjuring a thousand horrors that could be lurking just outside this refuge.

I long to be brave, to have the courage of all those stories and movies. But at this moment, I am small. I am afraid. My hands tremble, so I wrap my arms tight around my legs, trying to stop the shaking. But my heart continues to flutter like a frightened bird in my chest.

Thump thump. Thump thump. The rhythm of my fear drums relentlessly inside me. I squeeze my eyes shut, but that only makes it worse - the shadows seem to creep and flutter at the edges of my vision. I open them again quickly, staring into the dim light filtering under the door.

Is it my imagination, or are the footsteps getting closer? I hold my breath, listening with every fiber of my being. The footsteps pause, and muted voices murmur just on the other side of the door. I can't make out the words, but the tone sounds urgent and angry. My heart stutters and I must clap my hand over my mouth to contain a whimper.

They know I'm here. Any second, they could discover my hiding place. I'm trapped. Defenseless. There's nowhere to run. I can only wait helplessly for whatever horror is to come…

My thoughts race, jumping from one terrible possibility to the next. Are they soldiers, coming to take me away? Are they criminals, looking to loot and destroy? There is so much evil in the world right now, the danger could come from anywhere.

I strain to hear the voices again, hoping for some clue, some hint of who or what lurks right outside my fragile shelter.

But the words are too muffled, obscured by the thick door and my own ragged breathing.

Come on, I urge them silently. Say something I can understand. Give me some warning of what's about to happen. My mind spins scenarios, each more horrific than the last. Will they simply shoot through the door? Take an axe to it? Set the whole building on fire? Not knowing is agony.

I'm powerless, I realize. All I can do is wait here in paralyzed terror for whatever fate has in store. At least if I knew who or what I faced, I could prepare myself, and steel my courage for the confrontation ahead. But ignorant, all I can do is shudder in fear of the unknown evil to come.

The voices rise and fall in heated argument. I catch a few words here and there - "no choice," "orders," "family." None make any sense out of context. My mind races, grasping at meaning.

Then, a fragment cuts through with chilling clarity:

"The girl must be dealt with."

I freeze, heart hammering. Are they talking about me? But who are they? What do they want?

More indistinct arguing follows. I press desperately against the door, straining to hear. Suddenly, a voice rings out, cold and commanding.

"Enough!" he barks. "I gave you an order. The girl is a threat. You know what needs to be done."

I reel with shock. I am insignificant. They can't be talking about me. Yet they are so close.

An icy void opens within me. All certainty, all trust, drains away. I'm alone, with enemies on all sides. No one can be relied on - no one at all.

The man continues, oblivious to the devastation of his words.

"Go now. And no mistakes this time."

His footsteps recede down the hall, each one a hammer blow. I huddle in darkness, a girl alone against the world. I have only myself now. No one else can be trusted.

I sit paralyzed, struggling to breathe. My chest constricts as if crushed by a vice. I dig my fingernails into my palms, desperate for something to anchor me amidst the roiling chaos.

The implications cascade through me. No one is safe. Everything is uncertain. I can't even trust my own judgment - I can no longer see where the danger is coming from or who it is for. It is just all-encompassing.

I think of my family and my friends. Are they in danger too? Could he have been talking about them, about me? He could hunt us down, one by one. Fear and fury war within me. I want to scream, confront the murderer, and demand answers. But I'm powerless, hidden, and alone. All I can do is endure the torturous uncertainty.

Outside, muffled voices confer in ominous tones. I can't make out the words, but their meaning is clear - they must be coming for me. I am out of time.

I steady my breathing and clear my mind. If I'm to survive, I must find strength within myself. No one will save me now. I am the only one I can truly rely upon.

My thoughts race, each more terrifying than the last. I replay every interaction with every stranger I have ever met, searching for clues I missed. That day outside the school, when someone spoke to me to "ask how my family was doing". Was that a ruse to get information? Or the time someone brought gifts, acting as the doting guardian. Were those trinkets bugged?

I think of the secrets I confessed, seeking counsel from a mentor. The insights into my family I shared over cups of tea. Had someone harvested it all? Every weakness and fear laid bare for others to exploit. Were they Hamas all that time and I just didn't know? Danger was lurking everywhere, but nowhere did it run as rampant as in the dark corners of my mind.

Bile rises in my throat as I realize - I could have been the one who led the wolf to our door. My trust pried open our defenses and gave him the power to destroy everything I hold dear.

But why? What possible reason could justify such cruelty? I rack my brain but find no answer. Perhaps he simply enjoys wielding that power over us. We were chess pieces to maneuver in some twisted game only he understands.

Outside, floorboards creak under heavy boots. I imagine them searching from room to room, drawing inevitably closer. There will be nowhere to run soon.

I am well and truly alone now. I cannot even trust my own heart - it led me down this catastrophic path. My faith in others has always been my undoing. Now I must find faith in myself or perish.

Drawing my knees to my chest, I retreat deep within, steeling myself for whatever comes next. If this is to be my end, I will face it on my own terms, with courage.

Let them come for me. I am ready.

My breath catches as the footsteps stop outside the hidden door. I squeeze my eyes shut, willing my frantic heart to slow. This may be the end, but I refuse to cower.

A tense minute passes, and then the footsteps recede down the hall. I release a shaky exhale. A temporary reprieve - they will return soon enough.

I glance around the tiny space that has become my whole world. Blank walls offer no answers, no escape. I am well and truly trapped.

Trapped physically perhaps, but my mind remains free. I close my eyes once more and steady my breathing. Fear will not rule me. I let my thoughts drift back to better times - Mama's smile, Papa's laugh, my little brother's sticky hand in mine. My baby brother's smile. The memories wrap around me like a warm blanket, soothing my spirit.

War has taken so much, but it cannot take what lives on here. My memories, my inner light - those I keep safe. Darkness may close in, but it will never extinguish the flame within.

I straighten my spine and lift my chin, determination rising. Whatever comes, I am ready. My life is my own, and I will cling to it fiercely, for as long as I can.

CHAPTER XI

The booms ricochet through the cramped room, each one making my heart seize. I hold my diary closer, the cover creased under my white-knuckled grip. Eyes squeezed shut, I try to block out the muffled shouts, the cracks of gunfire. Just breathe, I tell myself. In and out. You can do this.

I open my eyes, blinking against the dim bulb overhead. With trembling fingers, I open to a blank page. The crisp sheet stares up at me, waiting. This is my chance to tell our story, to make sure we're remembered. Slowly, I poise my pen over the paper.

Another explosion rocks the room, closer this time. I flinch, a tear splashing onto the page. The walls feel like they're closing in on me. I can hardly breathe. My hand shakes as I force it to move, etching out the first words.

"Dear Anne,

Today, the bombs came again. I don't know how much more I can take. Some days, it feels like I'm the only one left. I'm trying to be strong like you were. You never gave up hope. But sometimes, I just want to hide under the mattress and cry.

I don't know if anyone will ever read this. Maybe someday, when all of this is over. Maybe someday, they'll understand what we sacrificed. What we endured. I must believe it will mean something.

For now, all I can do is keep writing. Bear witness. Pray that I make it through another night..."

I pause, blinking back tears as another round of explosions rocks the shelter. My hand continues to shake as I keep writing.

"I pretend I can hear others here with me, in bunks all around me, tossing and turning. No one can sleep through the bombardment. We're all just waiting, listening for the next blast, wondering if this will be the one that breaches our shelter.

I fear the worst. Our community is being torn apart, one explosion at a time. Families separated. Friends lost. And still, the shells keep falling.

I cling to my diary like a lifeline, the only thing keeping me tethered amidst the chaos. As long as I can put pen to paper, I have a purpose. I'm more than just a scared girl, hiding underground. I'm a voice crying out in the darkness, determined to be heard. My voice blends with yours Anne, mine from below, yours from far above, but both with the same fears and trauma, melting into one despairing silent scream.

We are more than statistics. We are human beings with stories that deserve to be told. I want people to know who we were - our hopes, dreams, fears. The little moments that made life worth living. Sharing an orange with my brother. Stargazing on the kibbutz roof. My first kiss, stolen behind the chicken coop..."

Another blast, closer still. The light flickers. I hold my breath, gripping my pen tightly.

"We will endure this. We must. I will write our stories, so the world remembers. Maybe someday, the guns will fall silent. And we can step out into the light once more.

The pounding reverberates through the concrete walls, but I barely flinch anymore. This shelter is my whole world now. I've lost track of how many days I've been down here. Time blurs together in the windowless gloom, measured only by the sporadic booms above.

My imagined friends huddled close on the cold, hard concrete, faces gaunt and pale beneath the one solitary light.

We wait in resigned silence.

But there is still strength here. I imagine my mother gently stroking my brother's hair as he sleeps, a protector to the last. Our teacher walks the aisle between beds, squeezing a shoulder here, and offering a weak smile there. Small gestures of comfort mean everything. In my dreams and imagination, I am not facing this alone. And of course, there is always you, Anne. A beacon of hope and strength in my darkness.

We are diminished, but not yet broken. The bonds of the community hold firm, even as our world fractures around us. Outside, there is only chaos and fear. But here, we have each other.

As long as I cling to that – as long as we remember who we are – hope remains. I will write of courage and sacrifice. I will tell our story, so it is never forgotten. We few who huddle in darkness, awaiting the light.

I look at my diary held in dirty, small hands, the pen heavy and unsure. Where to even begin? How to capture the full extent of the devastation above? My words feel so small in the face of such enormous loss.

But I must try. I must find a way to honor the dead, to paint a true picture of their suffering.

So, I write of the young mother who shields her baby with her own body, struck down by shrapnel just outside the bunker doors. The child's cries echoing through my shelter for hours, inconsolable in his grief. I imagine rocking him in my arms until his screams go silent. I don't want to think about what abruptly silenced his cries causing the tears to stream down my face.

I write about the teacher who volunteered to run for supplies, knowing the risk, dodging gunfire, and determined to provide for us all. Only silence returned.

Their names fill the pages. Neighbors, friends - all gone too soon. I do not have the words to give meaning to their loss. But I will not let their lives be reduced to statistics. If I can capture even a fraction of who they were, then their light will endure.

My hand cramps, but I push on. I write of the dwindling rations and my fraying nerves. But also, of the strength I draw from my little imagined group of refugees. The way we support those who falter, hold fast to hope when it gutters low.

We walked through the fire and somehow emerged whole. Scarred, shaken - but unbroken. Our stories are intertwined, bound by this shared trauma.

I will be the vessel to carry all their stories forward. Although some imagined, they are bound in fact, forged in fire, by the sounds and smells just outside my captive doorway.

I nod off as I write, the pen slipping from my fingers. I jerk awake, disoriented. The air is thick with smoke and the acrid stench of burnt metal.

My heart pounds. How long was I asleep? Minutes? Hours? It's impossible to tell in this windowless tomb. I strain to hear any sound besides the drone of the ventilation system.

Silence. The worst sound of all.

I force stiff fingers to resume writing. To put words to the nameless dread coiling in my gut.

"I have not heard from anyone for what I think is at least two, maybe three days now. Have they survived the latest bombardment? Or am I the only one left?

I want to believe help will come. That freedom and peace are more than fantasies danced before my eyes to keep me docile.

But belief is a luxury when each moment could be your last. When you've seen the mangled bodies and haunted eyes of those who prayed for deliverance that never arrived.

So, I will write while I still can. And if these pages are someday found, this record will speak for us. Will shout from beyond the grave the stories of those lost. We existed. We mattered. We were here."

I let the pen fall and flex my aching fingers. This cramped shelter allows little room to stretch weary muscles. I long to feel sunlight on my skin, to breathe air untainted by fear.

But those days seem lifetimes ago.

I stare at the final paragraph, rereading the shaky letters. What more is there to say? I wait, subsisting on dwindling hope, as the world collapses above me. This war has raged for so long now that I cannot recall peace. Only bloodshed and heartbreak.

There is a soft click as I close the diary. I slide it back into its hiding spot, fingers lingering on the worn cover. A piece of me lives within those pages now. My truth, borne of terror and longing.

If I do not survive, perhaps my words will. A flickering candle against the darkness. Proof that I was here. That I felt joy, pain, sorrow. That I loved.

For now, that purpose must sustain me.

I stand, joints creaking in protest, and make my way to the door. As I press my ear against the metal, I hear nothing. The fight continues, as it has every hour of every day, but the silence is the worst.

We persevere in hope. And though my hope falters, I force one foot in front of the other. Take each breath as it comes.

Outside this safe room, the battle rages on. But within me, there is still light.

I pause with my hand on the door handle, steeling myself. Pretending I can just open it and step into the sunshine. The muffled sounds from above are a grim reminder of what awaits. Gunfire. Screaming. The acrid smell of smoke and death. My heart hammers an anxious beat in my chest.

Just one more day, I beg silently. Let me see one more dawn.

This is how I mark time now. One breath, one heartbeat, one day at a time. My thoughts stray to Mama, wondering if she has found safety. If my remaining brother still draws breath. We are scattered like leaves, but the bonds of love persist.

I wish I could see the sun again.

I take a deep, shuddering breath and turn the handle. The heavy door swings open with a groan. I'm blinded for a moment as dust-filtered light spills in. Gunfire sounds in the distance. My eyes adjust. Desolation and loneliness have taken their toll. I must look outside if only for a moment. I am no longer immobilized by fear. I have become numb.

The safe room is one of many that dot the kibbutz, linked by a web of tunnels. It's eerily quiet down here. Most of the others are topside, taking their turn to fight. To try and protect our home.

I make my way through the winding passage, flashlight in hand. My footsteps seem unnaturally loud. I pass storerooms, and living quarters carved from the earth. All empty now.

I emerge topside behind the main house, next to the barn. The air is hazy with smoke, the smell of it acrid in my throat. I blink grit from my eyes and take in the scene. Fires smolder in the distance. The livestock barn - what remains of it - is a charred ruin. Swollen, burnt, animals — lifeless. The motionless body of an infant, its head ripped from the torso. This is not my home. Where am I?

In the west, tracer fire lights up the night sky. I say a silent prayer for those on the perimeter. The ones who stand between us and oblivion.

I spot a few others moving between buildings, rifles ready. Haunted looks on their faces. We are the prey here, scurrying for cover while death rains from above. It wasn't always like this. What hell am I witnessing? I ran back to my tiny haven, vowing never to come out again.

CHAPTER XII

The door slams shut behind me as I stumble into the safe room, the echo reverberating in my bones. My breath comes in ragged gasps, my heart hammering against my ribs. Muffled explosions and screams filter through the thick walls, each one making my body jolt. I sink to the floor, clutching my diary to my chest like a shield.

My hands tremble as I flip open the worn pages. The familiar looping script anchors me amidst the chaos. I clutch my pen tightly, etching each word deliberately across the paper.

"The noises are getting louder. I don't know how much longer I can last."

My eyes blur with tears. I blink them away. I must keep writing.

"I wish I could see a blue sky one more time. Feel the sun on my face."

A particularly close blast shakes the walls. I flinch, my pen slipping. A tear splashes onto the page, smearing the ink.

I take a shuddering breath. In and out. I can't lose it now. My diary is the only thing keeping me sane.

"Anne, you made it through this. I can too. I have to believe that."

The pen continues dancing across the page, transcribing my hopes and fears within its lines. Each word is a lifeline, connecting me to the world outside this cramped space.

My hand trembles with effort but I push on. I must. I repeat the words that have sustained me thus far. As long as I can write, I know I will survive this.

I pause, staring at the page. My thoughts drift to Mama and Papa. Are they safe? Have they found shelter?

I imagine Mama's slender frame huddled in a corner, her blue eyes wide with fear. Papa's strong arms wrapped around her, shielding her from harm.

My heart aches picturing them out there alone. I wish I could see their faces one more time. Hear their voices whisper that everything will be okay.

Instead, all I have is a pounding in my ears. The shuddering walls. The choking isolation.

I press my palms to my eyes, willing the tears away. Crying won't help them now. I need to be strong. Like Papa.

With a deep breath, I put pen to paper again:

"Mama, Papa – I hope you're safe. Stay strong for me. I _love_ you both so much. We'll get through this, I know it."

I underline "love" for emphasis. My hands shake but I steady them. I must be their voice now. Their lifeline.

Anne wrote to keep her loved ones close. Now I must do the same. These pages will tell Mama and Papa that I'm still here, still fighting.

That one day we'll all be together again. A family.

The explosions continue but I block them out, focusing only on the diary in my hands. Concentrating only on my words to Mama and Papa.

This is how I'll survive. This is how I'll see them again. Through the hope in my pen strokes. The love in the ink.

The walls shudder again, jolting me back to the agonizing present. I can't block it out anymore. Can't pretend this is all some nightmare I'll wake up from.

This is real. The explosions, the screams - it's all real. And my family is out there, somewhere in the chaos. Are they crouched in some dark room too, willing the madness to end? Or are they...

No. I can't think of it. I won't.

But the images push into my mind anyway. Mama's body, broken and bloodied in the street. Papa being dragged away

by men with guns. Their lives extinguished in an instant,
just like that poor baby I saw yesterday. Its' tiny head…

A sob escapes my throat before I can stop it. I hug my knees
to my chest, making myself small. Willing myself invisible.
But I can't un-see it. That limp little body. I imagine the
screams of the wailing mother. The horrors I've witnessed
repeat in my mind.

And now Mama and Papa are out there too. Are they safe?
Will I ever know? I'm helpless, useless - I can't protect
them. Can't stop this madness.

All I can do is sit here, writing in this diary like everything is
normal. But it's not. It never will be again.

I want to scream but force my lips shut. I must stay quiet.
Stay hidden.

The explosions continue. The nightmare rages on. And I'm
trapped here, alone with the visions I can't escape.

The pen shakes in my hand as I try to put words to the chaos in my mind. My neighbors, the Goldsteins, the Cohens, the Levines - are they hunkered down somewhere too? Enduring the same fear that claws at my insides?

I think of the Goldsteins' laughter floating from their kitchen window as we shared Shabbat dinner not long ago. Little Sarah Levine's joyful giggles as we played hopscotch. The way old Mr. Abramowitz's face crinkled into a smile when he told stories of the old country.

These are the memories I cling to. Proof that not long ago, our lives were normal. Happy, even. That the monsters haven't taken everything from us. Not yet.

We must be strong, like the mighty trees that lined our street. Sturdy trunks weathering the hurricane. I think of the young mother who shielded her baby with her own body when the mortars fell. The teenager who helped pull survivors from the rubble, heedless of the danger. My people are survivors. We have endured so much.

But even the strongest trees can break in the fiercest storms. I've now seen the hollow, haunted eyes of my neighbors, like ghosts wandering the streets. Heard the muffled sobs behind closed doors as we all waited for this to end. We're battered and bent, but not yet broken.

There is still hope. Still love. I must believe that.

So, I will keep writing, and keep holding onto the memories of laughter and joy. Of better times that will come again. And when this darkness lifts, we will stand tall once more, our branches reaching towards the light.

I stare at the many empty pages left in my diary, struggling to find the words. How can I capture the full weight of this suffering on paper? The pen trembles in my hand.

I think of Anne, scribbling away in her tiny attic, searching for light amidst the darkness. Did she feel this same paralysis? This crushing helplessness and fear?

My situation mirrors hers in so many ways. Hidden away in a cramped room while violence rages right outside the door. Worrying endlessly about loved ones I can't reach. Trying to hold onto hope when it feels so far away.

She found the courage to keep writing even as the Nazis tightened their grip on Amsterdam. Her words are a lifeline, helping me make sense of my own pain. No one else can truly understand what this feels like.

I envy the comfort she took in imagining a dear friend reading her diary after the war ended. But I have no Kitty. No one I can fully confide in. The solitude is suffocating.

Still, Anne persevered. So, must I. If I can't ease this suffering, perhaps I can at least bear witness. Honor the stories of those who endured these horrors before me.

One day, I hope someone will read these pages. They'll know we cling to our humanity, even now. We have so much left to do, to feel, to be. I can't let that be taken from me. From any of us.

So, I will keep writing. For them. For me. For the futures we are all still fighting for.

My hands tremble as I grip my pen, the dim bulb making it hard to see the pages. How long have I been huddled here in the dark? Minutes stretch into hours with no way to tell one from the next.

The muffled sounds from outside taunt me - shouts and screams, explosions in the distance. Each one makes my heart race faster. Are they getting closer? How much more can the walls take before they crumble?

I squeeze my eyes shut, trying to block it all out. But the images are still etched into my mind. The wailing child clutching her mother's limp body. My neighbor's home collapsed in a pillar of smoke. Hamas terrorists in trucks, dragging young men, women, and children from their families.

When will it end? When will we know peace again?

I long for the simple comforts - a warm meal with loved ones, the embrace of my mother, the laughter of friends. Things I took for granted are now gone.

My thoughts drift to my family. Are they huddled in darkness too, praying to make it through another night? I pray they're together, keeping each other's spirits up. Imagining them gives me strength. For them, I will hold on.

The waiting tears me apart. I want to run into the streets and scream for this madness to stop! But I'm trapped here - useless, helpless. My pen is the only weapon I have left.

So, I write into the lonely night, spilling my anguish onto these pages. One more candle lit against the spreading darkness. One more voice begging for the bloodshed to end.

They will hear us someday. The world will know we did not go quietly. We persisted, despite everything.

This cannot last forever. The light will come again. It must.

The pounding at the door startled me from my writing. I freeze, listening. Angry shouts in a language I don't understand. They're searching the building. It's only a matter of time before they find me.

I hold on to my diary, my final refuge. On these pages I've poured my soul, leaving a piece of me behind in case I don't make it through this night.

The sounds draw nearer. Heavy boots on the floors above. Furniture crashes as they toss the rooms. Coming for me.

A tear splashes on the page, blurring the ink. I brush it away hastily. No time for tears now. I must be strong.

Bowing my head, I whisper a prayer. For courage, for those I love, for an end to this madness. Let us see the dawn.

The doorknob rattles. This is it. I steel myself, holding fast to my faith. If this is my final hour, let me face it with dignity.

They will not take my spirit, no matter what comes. I am more than flesh and blood. My story lives on in these pages. I will persist.

The end comes crashing through the door. I lift my head high, diary clasped to my heart. I am ready.

The door bursts open and I flinch, bracing for the worst. Heavy boots thunder across the floor. I squeeze my eyes shut, clutching my diary like a shield. I feel my grip on reality loosening.

But the anticipated blow doesn't come. Instead, a familiar voice cries out, "Rachel! Thank God!"

My eyes fly open to see my father rushing toward me. I'm enveloped in his strong arms before I can comprehend what's happening.

"Papa!" I sob into his shoulder, the diary tumbling from my hands.

He holds me tight, stroking my hair. "You're safe now, baby girl. I've got you."

I weep with relief. My prayers were answered. My father is alive, and he found me.

Footsteps approach and I look up to see my mother, her face streaked with tears. She joins our embrace. For a long moment, we just hold each other, rocking gently.

Together again, against all odds. My family, my heart - still beating. There is hope after all.

I retrieve my diary from the floor and pick it up once more. But the words inside no longer hold the same urgency. This is no longer my sole refuge or a vessel for my fading voice.

My story continues, surrounded by the loving arms of my family. And though darkness still reigns outside, in this moment, there is light. My baby brother smiles up at me…

And then, I awaken.

CHAPTER XIII

I jump from the mattress, heart hammering. For a moment, I think I still hear Mama and Papa's voices. But the room is empty, the air still. Just another cruel trick of my imagination. It was nothing more than a dream. I collapse. I curse God. Down here even my deepest dreams are shattered in an instant. Reality sets in quickly through the fog of waking.

I'm alone. I must rely on myself now.

My eyes dart around the dim safe room, taking in the bare walls and the pile of musty blankets in the corner. Somewhere in here, there might be something I can use. Food. Pens. Anything.

I slid off the mattress, wincing as my feet hit the cold concrete floor. The pounding in my chest echoes in my ears as I creep along the edges of the small space. I run my hands over the rough walls, feeling for any hidden nooks or crannies.

I think of my family and my friends. Are they safe? Hungry like me? I swallow hard, pushing the thoughts away. Focus on now.

For today, I will have hope.

It's enough to keep me alive. And if I'm alive, I can endure this. I make myself believe that.

I return to my diary, pen poised. The words pour out in a jumble - my hopes, my fears, my will to go on. Anne Frank's words echo in my mind:

"In spite of everything, I still believe people are good at heart." (Frank, 1991)

I cling to that belief like a lifeline, even now. There is cruelty and chaos in this world, yes. But there is also kindness, beauty, and love. If I can find the light again someday, then I must not give up.

With renewed energy, I continue writing. The pen is an anchor, my diary a friend. If I have words, I have a reason to survive another day.

Step by step, hour by hour, I will endure this. Darkness cannot last forever. The light will return. I only need to hold on until it does.

There is hope still, I will survive. My will remains unbroken, my spirit unbowed. I will go on. I must believe that better days will come again. For now, I am still here. Still breathing. Still surviving.

It is enough.

I nod, steeling myself. Enough wallowing in fear. I have work to do.

Methodically, I search the safe room, looking for anything useful. Extra clothes, tools, books - all may prove valuable. I check under the mattress and peel back the edges of the worn rug. My eyes land on a small wooden box in the corner of the room.

Slowly, I lift the lid. My breath catches as I reach inside. My fingers brush something hard and cold. Metal.

I pull it out with trembling hands - a small tin. Dare I hope? Hands fumbling, I pry off the lid.

Crackers. Packets upon packets of crisp, salty crackers. My mouth waters at the sight. And a half-full bottle of water!

"Thank you," I whisper to the empty room, to whoever left this gift. Tears prick my eyes. With this, I can last a little longer.

I allow myself one package of crackers, savoring the taste of the two precious wafers. The water soothes my throat as I take small sips. I eat slowly, making it last. Rationing. This must sustain me for who knows how long.

But for now, I feel renewed hope stirring within. This changes everything. With this discovery, I can continue my fight to survive another day. Step by step, moment by moment, I am still fighting.

I carefully replace the lid, concealing my precious discovery once more. No need to risk anyone else finding my hidden treasure. This will be my secret, my lifeline.

Settling back on the mattress, I retrieve my diary and pen. The familiar weight of the book in my hands anchors me yet again, like an old friend. I document my last meal - however long ago that was. Days? Weeks? Time blurs here.

Now I can write about this gift I've found. Proof that even in darkness, there are glimmers of light if you know where to look. My words transform despair into hope. I cling to that hope with all that I have left. After the cruel dreams of last night, I am hanging on to my sanity by a thin thread.

My pen scratches swiftly, etching today's events into memory. The empty pages await my future. However long or short that may be, I will face it as I have everything since coming here - with courage, faith, and determination.

I may be trapped here, but my mind remains free. And through my words, I find freedom. My diary bears witness to all that happens, and all that is within me. On these pages, I live.

For now, this is enough. My semi-full belly and the words
flowing from my pen grant me a pocket of peace amidst the
chaos beyond this room. I breathe deeply, cherishing this
moment of light before bracing myself for the darkness to
come. But I do not despair. Not anymore. Not when I have
my pen, my diary, and the hope that lives on in me.

The cracker crumbs stick in my throat as I swallow, tasting
of cardboard yet infinitely better than the gnawing
emptiness of before. My stomach rumbles, not used to such
bounty after so long without. I eat slowly, carefully,
knowing I must make each bite last, but I am so famished.
Who knows when I will find such fortune again?

With food comes strength, and energy - dangerous things
when despair has been your companion. My mind, dulled by
hunger, sharpened by necessity, begins to wander. To my
family, my friends, my classmates. Are they still out there?
Have they found safety and sustenance? Or do they suffer as
I do, lost and alone?

I picture my mother's face - careworn, eyes sunken with
worry and sleepless nights. My father's strong arms which
once enveloped me in hugs, are now weakened by the lack
of food. My little brother's bright laughter silenced; his eyes
dulled by horrors no child should see.

Are they searching for me even now? Scouring the rubble, calling my name with voices raw from smoke and ash? Or am I but a memory, mourned and missed but slowly fading with each passing day?

My heart aches with every beat. I squeeze my eyes shut, fighting back the sting of tears. I want to go home. I want my old life back - lazy weekends, school plays, family dinners. Not this never-ending nightmare.

But home is gone. The life I knew burnt up in flames. I can't dwell in the past or I'll lose myself to despair. Focus, Rachel. The present is all you have. Survive today so you might see tomorrow.

I steady my breathing and open my eyes. One more bite slowly chewed. The cracker is gritty on my tongue. My belly is getting almost full for the first time in what seems like forever. This is enough. This is everything.

I will endure this. I must believe I will see them again. Until then, I have my pen, my pages, and the hope that lives on through my words. I am still here. I am still fighting. I will not give up.

The last crumbs cling to my fingers as I savor them, not wanting to waste a single morsel. My body thrums with renewed energy, my mind clearer than it's been in days. I feel almost human again.

I know it won't last. Hunger is a constant companion, gnawing away no matter how much I eat. But for now, I'll embrace this moment of fullness. This reprieve from the hollow ache inside.

Carefully, I slide the box back into place again, vowing not to get into it again until tomorrow, concealing my precious cache once more. I smooth my hands over the wood, erasing any sign of disturbance. My secret, my salvation, hidden away once more.

My palms tingle when they touch the cool tin. I imagine the can, waiting there patiently for the next time I need it. A loyal friend sharing his strength.

The room feels less oppressive now. Shadows retreat to the corners as dim light filters through from the perimeter of the door. I blink, letting my vision adjust.

What now? I could reread my diary, tracing memories inked on the pages. Or continue writing, spinning dreams of the future. For the first time in forever, I feel hope stirring within.

This changes nothing, yet everything. I'm still trapped, still fighting to survive. But I'm not ready to give up. Not yet. If hope remains, so will I.

I settle onto the thin mattress, my diary resting on bent knees. The binding creaks a little as I open it, the sound comforting and familiar. My fingers trail over the margins, crammed with thoughts and dreams. So many words spilled on these pages, charting my journey through darkness into light.

Pen once again poised over paper, I ponder where to begin. What to write about this small triumph of discovery. My cramped script marches onward, bearing witness to my days. There is always room for more.

Each word is a brick in the fortress I'm building. Protecting the kernel of hope I've found. My writing wraps around me like a blanket, shielding me from stark reality. In these pages, I am safe. I have a voice.

Anne Frank's words echo in my mind:

"I want to go on living even after my death." (Frank, 1991)

As long as this diary survives, some piece of me will live on. My experiences won't vanish into the void.

I press the pen down, watching the ink bleed into the fibrous paper. Today, I choose to hope. To believe I can endure this. That there are still glimmers of light worth writing about.

My hand trembles, but I keep writing. One word leads to the next, a lifeline pulling me forward. I am still here. Still fighting. My story continues, as long as I keep writing it.

CHAPTER XIV

I sit up with a gasp, the echoes of bombs and gunfire still ringing in my ears. I must have passed out from my much-needed, meager meal and the exhaustion that followed. Was it a dream? Even my dreams are now betraying me. There is nothing left. The dusty air of the safe room fills my lungs as I try to slow my frantic breaths. I'm alone. Utterly alone. But as my gaze drifts to the corner, the little wooden box is still there. It was real!

My fingers tremble as I reach for the worn leather diary resting beside me. The one place I can still visit the ghosts of the past.

With a shaky exhale, I open to a blank page. My pen hovers, hesitant. Why should I even bother? How can mere words capture the kaleidoscope of memories and emotions churning inside me? I curse God for making me doubt my dreams too, I can't find relief anywhere.

"I close my eyes, picturing the sun-filled kitchen on a lazy Saturday morning. The smell of challah in the oven is rich and sweet.

Papa sitting at the table, newspaper in hand, while Mama gathers ingredients for our Shabbat meal.

Their voices, warm with love and teasing, float back to me.

"Such a good helper, my Rachel," Mama says, dropping a kiss on my hair.

I grin, whisking the batter with youthful enthusiasm. Little do I know this moment of peace is already slipping away, as fragile as a soap bubble floating on the breeze."

The pen slides across the page, etching the memory into my heart. If I can hold on to these fragments, perhaps I can survive the desolation surrounding me.

My stomach rumbles, ignored. I must conserve my little culinary treasure. Time bleeds together in the windowless gloom.

I tuck the diary away, curling myself into a ball. Sleep is my only escape, however brief. My dreams still brim with light and hope, even as my reality fractures into darkness once I awaken.

I cling to the belief that someday, somehow, the light will return. And my family will be whole once more.

The memory shifts, and I'm transported back to lazy summer days playing in the yard with my brother Daniel. He's two years younger, with a mop of unruly curls and a grin missing two front teeth. We'd spend hours chasing each other around the old oak tree, its branches draped like a protective canopy above us.

I squeal as he tackles me into the soft grass, both of us collapsing into breathless giggles. No matter how many times I pin him down, he wiggles free and takes off again. His energy is boundless.

"You can't catch me, I'm too fast!" he taunts playfully.

My competitive spirit rising, I tear after him determinedly. I always let him win in the end. His joyous laughter as he pumps his fists in victory are reward enough.

After, we sprawl on the ground gazing up at the clouds. He points to a fluffy bunny shape or soaring bird, spinning colorful stories about their adventures. His imagination is so vibrant. Mine pales in comparison.

In the golden glow of carefree days, we feel invincible. If only I could shield his innocence from the horrors to come. My heart aches, not knowing where he is now…or if I'll ever see him again.

But I must cling to hope. It's all I have left.

My breath catches as I turn the page of my diary. Eitan's face smiles up at me, his green eyes dancing with amusement. I trace my fingers over his face, transported back to that sunny afternoon at the park.

We sit on the swings, legs dangling, as we swap stories of school and family. His dry wit makes me erupt in laughter again and again. I find myself opening up to this kind, thoughtful boy I have just met.

As the day goes on, we discover our shared love of art and poetry. I show him my sketches, cheeks flaming red, but he studies each one intently before proclaiming them "brilliant." We recite verses from our favorite poems, our voices mingling in perfect harmony.

At that moment, I felt a profound connection. Here is someone who truly sees past my shy exterior to the creative soul within. I sense he feels it too from the way his gaze lingers on mine.

Just then, a gruff voice calls Eitan's name. We turn to see a stern-faced soldier approaching, his uniform starkly militaristic.

"Time to go," the soldier commands. Eitan nods, rising slowly.

As he walks away, he glances back at me, regret shadowing his face. In that look, I see longing that mirrors my own.

If only we lived in a different world, I think wistfully. One where we could be together without fear.

The make-believe memory fades as I open my eyes to the cold reality of the safe room. Gray concrete walls and the lingering scent of dust.

My fingers drift to the gold locket at my neck, tracing the delicate Star of David engraving. It was a gift for my bat mitzvah, the last celebration we had as a family before the war broke out.

I see Bubbe bustling about the kitchen, cheeks flushed as she checks the brisket in the oven. Her eyes crinkle with joy as Zayde hoists me onto his shoulders so I can affix the streamers. Mama and Papa sway to the music lost in each other's gaze.

The house was filled with so much love and warmth that day. I remember thinking we'd always be together, that nothing could ever tear apart our family.

How naive I was.

Now, Mama and Papa are gone. Probably taken away by the terrorists or worse, their imagined screams still echo in my dreams. Bubbe and Zayde's fate is unknown, no word since they were forced from their home.

And Daniel…my sweet, mischievous brother, only ten years old when he was ripped from my arms. I cling to the belief that he's still out there, somewhere. That I'll find him again one day.

It's memories of that joyous, untroubled time that sustain me now. They remind me what I'm fighting for - a chance to regain even a fraction of that love and light we once knew.

So, I will go on documenting our struggle in these pages, bearing witness to the evil that has shattered so many lives. And I will keep hope alive that someday, somehow, we will be whole again.

I take a deep, shuddering breath as I close my diary. The tears come unbidden, streaming down my cheeks. I make no effort to wipe them away.

Here, alone in this cramped safe room that has become my whole world, I finally let the full weight of my loss crash over me. It's too much to bear.

My family, my friends - all gone. Scattered to the winds or worse. I may never see them again. Never hear Papa's booming laugh or feel Mama's gentle hand on my cheek. Never see the mischief sparkling in Daniel's eyes or feel Bubbe pull me into a warm, floury embrace.

The life I knew has been ripped away, leaving a gaping wound that throbs with each beat of my heart. I yearn for the simplicity of the past before this brutal war tore our world apart.

But I know I cannot dwell there. I must be strong, as strong as Zayde facing down the Cossacks, as resilient as Bubbe starting over in a strange new land. Their courage is my courage now.

I stand on shaky legs, steadying myself against the wall. Wiping the last dampness from my eyes, I move toward the heavy door.

It is time. My companions are waiting. Together, we will face whatever comes next.

I take a deep, shuddering breath and slide open the heavy metal latch. The door creaks open and I step out into the dimly lit hallway where my imagined companions wait.

Their faces are grim, eyes shadowed with fear and exhaustion. We have survived together in this bunker for weeks, but our food is running low, and the water pump is failing. We cannot hide here much longer.

Avi's expression is stern as always, his jaw tight beneath his greying beard. But I can see the weariness in the sag of his broad shoulders. Even this battle-hardened soldier is reaching his limit.

Beside Avi stands Eitan, tall and lean, his curly dark hair disheveled. He gives me a faint smile, but it doesn't reach his somber green eyes. My dear friend who once made me laugh so easily now rarely even speaks.

We gather silently, needing no words to express what we all know - the time has come to leave this fragile shelter. If we stay, we starve. If we go outside, the dangers are unimaginable.

I finger the fraying pages of my diary, drawing courage from the inky testament I have made here. Come what may, I will continue to write, to remember, to hope.

With tentative steps, we make our way down the long corridor toward the heavy metal door that separates us from the world outside. A world that has become alien and threatening.

We glance at each other, bracing our nerves. Then, as one, we push open the door and step out into the unknown.

CHAPTER XV

My breath catches in my throat as I reenter the safe room, my escape thwarted by the sound of more gunfire in the distance, the heavy door sealing shut behind me with an ominous thud. The small space feels instantly claustrophobic, the bare walls and dim lightbulb amplifying my anxiety. I clutch my diary to my chest, its worn cover and frayed pages a small comfort in this familiar place.

Running my fingers over the diary, I open to a blank page. My hands tremble, making the pen jitter across the paper. I take a deep breath, trying to steady myself, to gather the courage to write. But the words spill out anyway, frantic and afraid.

"Where are you, Papa? Why haven't you come for me? What if something happened to you out there? What if I never see you again?"

Tears blur my vision as I write, smudging the ink.

"I imagine you bursting through the door, sweeping me up in your strong arms. I imagine your laugh, your smile, the safety of your embrace. Our home, before all this happened. Before they took you away."

But the door stays closed. The room is silent and still.

I'm alone, just me and these pages. Dark scenarios swirl in my mind, each one worse than the last. I cling to the diary, anchoring myself with its solid form. Hoping my words can keep the fear at bay. I hope that maybe, somehow, you will read them one day. And you'll know that I love you. That I miss you. That I'm still waiting for you, Papa. Still hoping you'll come back to me.

I take a shuddering breath, trying to steady my hand enough to keep writing. The pen wavers, my fingers cramping from how tightly I'm gripping it. But I need to get the words out before they consume me.

"Where are you? Why did they take you? What are they doing to you? The questions barrage my mind, each one a needle in my heart. I imagine the worst – that they've hurt you, that I'll never see your smile again. Never hear your voice. Never feel the comfort of your arms around me."

I write it all down, every dark thought and visceral fear. The pen flies across the page, my hand barely able to keep up with the torrent. Ink blots spread like bloodstains, tears falling to mingle with them.

"I plead over and over for you to come back to me, Papa. To be okay. To not leave me alone here, in this cold, foreign place."

But the pages are still silent, offering no answers. And the truth weighs heavier with each word – that I don't know where you are. That I might never see you again. A sob hitches in my throat as I write your name once more, screaming for you in my mind.

"Papa!"

My pen clatters on the concrete as it drops from my cramped fingers. I press the diary to my chest as if I can squeeze you from its pages.

"Come back to me, Papa," I whisper into the emptiness.

My voice was small and fragile, like the last flicker of hope within me. I squeeze my eyes shut, clinging to the diary like a lifeline, rocking gently back and forth. And wait for you to walk through that door. Silent tears stream down my face, dropping onto the cold hard floor.

I take a deep, shuddering breath, trying to calm the storm inside me. My hands tremble as I open the diary once more, staring at your smiling face on the inside cover. A photograph from simpler times.

"I remember the day it was taken – a warm summer afternoon at the park. You pushed me on the swings, higher and higher until I was soaring. I begged you not to let go. You just laughed and promised you never would.

We got ice cream after, chocolate dripping
down our fingers. You tried to wipe my face,
but I squirmed away, giggling. I wish I could
go back to that carefree girl, unfazed by the
dangers of this world.

Instead, I sit here, writing to ghosts. Hoping
my words can conjure you up, like a magical
incantation. Putting our memories on paper
might make them real again.

But the ink is still fixed in place. And you are
still gone. The photograph is all I have left.
Frozen moments of joy, trophies of a life
interrupted."

I trace your face with my finger. "I miss you, Papa," I
whisper. My vision blurs with fresh tears. All I can do is
wait, pen poised over the page, recording all that I've lost. I
hope beyond hope that you will come back to me.

The tears drip down onto the page, smudging the ink of
your smiling face. I quickly blot the photo dry, but the
damage is done. Your image blurs before me.

Why haven't you come for me? Where are you?

My mind conjures up terrible scenes - you are lying injured somewhere, crying out for help. Or worse, no longer breathing. No. I can't think like that. You must still be out there, fighting to get back to me.

But the Hamas' grip tightens by the day. I hear their feet running past my hiding place, barking orders. The world I know is disappearing.

I cling to the fading picture of you, the last remnant of my old life.

"If I lose this too, what will I have left? Who would I be without you to guide me?

The waiting eats away at me. How long until I'm found here? I imagine the door crashing open, the soldier's cruel shout."

My hand trembles, etching those fears onto the page.

Stay strong, I tell myself. Like a character in those books you gave me. Never lose hope.

But it flickers like a dying candle, guttering in the darkness. My pen moves feverishly, writing us the happy ending we deserve. Where you burst in and take me home.

For now, these pages are the only place we can still be together. My diary has become my only escape.

I will endure, as long as I can feel the brush of your hand on my shoulder. Hear your voice saying, "Everything will be alright."

I pause, listening. Only the pounding of my heart fills the silence.

"Where are you now? Are you thinking of me too? Do you whisper my name into the lonely night?

I imagine your warm embrace, your scratchy beard on my cheek. The smell of pipe smoke and cinnamon meant you were near."

My hands tremble, smudging the words. I blink back hot tears, clutching my pen like a lifeline.

Focus, Rachel. One word at a time. Write it all down so you won't forget.

I fill the next page with memories - your bellowing laugh, the songs you'd hum on the way to temple. The way you'd swing me up in your arms, spinning until we both got dizzy.

Those simple moments are treasures now. Each one is a talisman against the growing dark.

I run my fingers over the dried ink, over the impressions left by my desperate script. If the words remain, you are not completely lost to me.

My eyelids grow heavy, but I force them open. I must bear witness for both of us. To honor you by living, even in this limbo.

I will keep writing until there are no more pages. Until you return or the lights go out. My words will be waiting for whichever comes first.

I stare at the blank page, willing the right words to come. My pen hovers and dips, leaving scattered dots like breadcrumbs.

Where do I begin to capture the yawning chasm of your absence? How do I give shape to this aching loss?

I start slowly, fumbling my way forward.

"Dear Anne,

The days blur together in endless greys. I mark time by the imagined changing of the guards, and the irregular arrival of food. My world has shrunk down to this small room and the view from my imagination.

The mundane details feel insignificant, but my father taught me the importance of bearing witness. If I can't have you here, then I will conjure you through stories.

Does Papa remember that summer at the lake house, when he tried to teach me to fish? I feared the wriggling worms and got my line tangled. But he didn't get upset. He patiently untangled the line and baited the hook himself...

I lose myself in the memories, transported back to golden afternoons on the dock, the laughing arguments over Scrabble games, and Mama singing as we washed dishes side by side."

The stories pour out of me, a record of our lives together. Proof that what we had was real and meaningful, no matter what comes next.

My hand cramps, but I push past the pain. If I keep writing, a part of them survives. My words are a candle burning against the coming dark. An anchor holding me steady in the storm.

I may run out of stories eventually, but not yet. Not while their voices still echo in my mind. Not while hope remains.

The cramping in my hand grows more intense, but I barely notice it now. I'm lost in the memory of our trip to the fair last summer. How Papa laughed as I stubbornly refused to let go of that oversized stuffed panda I won at the ring toss. How we gorged on funnel cakes and candy apples, not caring about stomach aches or brain freezes.

My writing becomes more frantic as I try to capture every detail. The tinny jangle of carnival music, the sticky sweetness coating our fingers, the glint of joy in his eyes. I want to recreate that perfect day, to live in that moment forever.

The pages are filling fast, and my usually neat handwriting has gone sloppy and rushed. But I push on, wringing every drop from my memories. I strain to recall the sound of their voices, the cadence of Papa's laughter. Like trying to hold water in cupped hands, the details are slipping away no matter how tightly I grasp them.

Still, I write, fighting against the ache in my hand and the growing hollowness inside me. This diary is the only way I can still reach them, can keep them close. I pour my heart out onto the page, trusting that they will know me here even if we can't be together.

My hand spasms, finally forcing me to stop. I flex my stiff fingers as I stare down at the chaotic scrawl filling page after page after page. It's a frantic, disjointed mess, but somehow it captures this moment perfectly.

Closing the diary, I take a long slow breath. Though my heart still aches with uncertainty, sharing these memories lightens my spirit. If I remember, they're not fully gone.

I hold the diary close, feeling the embossed cover press against me. The worn blue leather is familiar, smooth under

my fingertips. Outwardly it is still pristine, but the pages
within bear the marks of my innermost thoughts.

After my hand has rested and with a deep breath, I open to a
blank page. The ivory sheet stares up at me, empty and
waiting. Waiting for the words I long to say but have no one
here to say them to.

My pen hovers over the paper as I gather my thoughts. So
much I want to express - fear, anger, grief. All the emotions
churning inside me with nowhere to go.

Finally, the dam breaks. My pen scratches frantically over
the paper as I pour it all out. Messy, chaotic - my true inner
world exposed raw on the page.

Tears drop, smearing the ink. I swipe at them angrily but it's
no use. Sorrow flows from my pen as freely as tears fall.
Still, I write on, purging my pain in the only way I can.

The pages fill, my outpouring of anguish having no end.
Still, it is not enough. But I persist, wringing every drop
from my aching heart until nothing is left.

Spent, I carefully close the diary once more. Cradling it to my chest, I feel a small sense of peace. My spirit is lighter having unburdened myself, if only on paper. It is but a temporary balm, yet it gives me the strength to continue waiting and hoping.

CHAPTER XVI

My breath catches in my throat as I stare at the empty mattress where Mama should be. I imagine the rumpled sheets of her bed from our home. Her pillow with the indentation of her head. But no Mama.

My hands tremble. I clench the diary to stop their shaking. Where is she? Did they find her hiding place? Take her away? Did she even make it to a safe space? Or worse…

I squeeze my eyes shut. No. I can't think of it. But the image forces its way into my mind - Mama lying lifeless on the ground. A dark stain spread across her dress. Her beautiful blue eyes are vacant.

A choked sob escapes me. My knees buckle and I sink to the floor. It can't be true. Not my Mama. She promised she would never leave me. Promised we would survive this together. She promised.

I take a gulping breath, trying to steady myself. But it's no use. Tears spill down my cheeks. I taste their salt on my lips.

Oh, Mama. My haven has become a trap. I'm all alone now. No one left to hold me and stroke my hair. To whisper that everything will be alright.

I don't know how to go on without you. My heart feels as if it's being ripped from my chest. All I want is to see your sweet face again. To hear your voice call my name.

I bury my face in the pillow, breathing in your lingering scent. Lavender and warmth. Home.

You can't be gone, Mama. You just can't.

I rock myself back and forth, arms wrapped around my knees. The silence presses down on me, suffocating. It's so quiet I can hear my ragged breaths.

What's the point of this diary now? No one will ever read it. My story will vanish just like Mama.

I glance at the door, at the sliver of light visible.

It's still light out. I should go search for her. But my limbs feel heavy, frozen. I'm too scared to move from this spot.

If I go out there and find the truth…it will break me. Shatter me into a million pieces. If I stay here, there's still a chance. Still a thread of hope to cling to.

But hope is slipping through my fingers no matter how tightly I grasp it. Deep down, I know. I've lost her. My heart, my home. Gone.

The tears come again, a great heaving sob that steals the breath from my lungs. I press my fist against my mouth to stop the screams I feel rising.

She promised we would always be together. She would never leave me. Oh god, how I wish I could see her face just one more time. To thank her for the endless love she gave me. I took it all for granted.

And now I have nothing. No one. I'm alone in this cold, dark world. The little girl in me wants to cry out for my Mama. But she isn't coming back. I know that now.

I must find a way to be strong on my own. But I don't know where to begin. My heart is shattered to dust.

The pounding in my head matches the frantic rhythm of my heart. I press my palms against my ears, trying to dull the noise. It doesn't help. My pulse is deafening.

I stagger to my feet, using the wall to steady myself. The room sways and blurs. When was the last time I ate or drank anything? I can't remember.

My legs are unsteady beneath me as I make my way to the door. I open the latch, wincing at the bright sunlight. It feels wrong that the world is still turning as normal.

Up on the street, I imagine that I see people passing by. Mundane errands are being run as if this were any other day. Don't they know my world has ended? Nothing will ever be the same. Is this real? Is this a dream?

I want to scream at them, to make them understand. But I remain silent, watching from my hidden doorway. They look happy, smiling at each other. I've forgotten what happiness feels like. I am dreaming, I must be.

A gnawing ache in my stomach reminds me I need to eat. But I can't. The thought of food makes me nauseous. There is not even room for one cracker. There's only one thing I need right now. And she's gone forever.

I let the door close again, shutting out the light. Maybe if I hide here long enough, I'll wake up from this nightmare. Or maybe I'll simply fade away into nothing. Both seem better than facing this harsh new reality.

I sink down onto the cold floor, wrapping my arms around my knees. Rocking slowly back and forth, I hum the lullaby she used to sing to me. The one that would always soothe me to sleep, no matter how scared I felt.

Sleep, sleep, my little girl.

Sleep, sleep.

Sleep, sleep, my little one,

Sleep, sleep.

Daddy's gone to work -

He went, Daddy went.

He'll return when the moon comes out -

He'll bring you a present!

Sleep, sleep…

Daddy went to the vineyards -

He went, Daddy went.

He'll return when the stars come out -

He'll bring you grapes!

Sleep, sleep…

Daddy went to the orchard -

He went, Daddy went.

He'll return in the evening with the wind -

He'll bring an apple!

Sleep, sleep…

Daddy went to the field -

He went, Daddy went.

He'll come back in the evening with the shadows -

He'll bring you ears of grain!

I wipe my eyes, but the tears keep coming. I'm crying so hard I can barely breathe. Gasping, I try to calm myself. But it's no use.

I need her. I've always needed her. Ever since I was little, she's been my rock, my safe place. I don't know how to do this without her.

Guilt wells up inside, hot and sickening. I should have protected her. I should have been there. If only I had stayed by her side. She'd still be here with me.

It's all my fault. I was too weak, too selfish. I let her down and now she's gone. The one person I loved more than anything in this world. The one person I needed most.

I thought we'd always have each other. She promised she would never leave me. Promised she'd always look out for her baby girl. But she broke that promise. And I'm all alone.

It's too much. I want to give up. What's the point of going on now? I have no one. I am no one without her. Just a scared little girl crying on the floor, wishing for her Mama to come back.

But she can't come back. And the little girl is gone too. There's only me now in this cold, empty room. Me and my guilt and my grief, swallowing me whole. My childhood was completely erased, as if it never existed.

I don't know how to do this. I don't know how to be alone. But I have no choice. I must find a way. I must be strong now. For her.

Somehow, I must carry on.

My hands won't stop shaking. I clench them into fists, trying to still the tremors, but it's no use. My whole body is quaking with fear, grief, and panic. I feel like I might shake apart and crumble to nothingness at any moment.

There's a tightness in my chest too, like a metal band cinched too tight, making it hard to breathe. Each inhale is a struggle. I gasp for air that won't fill my lungs.

I pace the small room, back and forth, back and forth. Looking for answers, for hope, finding none. Just four walls closing in on me, trapping me here alone.

Alone.

The word echoes through my mind. Bouncing off the inside of my skull. Reminding me.

She's not coming back. I'll never see her again. Never hear her voice. Feel her arms around me, holding me close. My mother. My whole world. Gone.

I imagine Hamas dragging her away. Her screams as they torture her. The gunshot. Her body going limp and cold.

No. Stop. I can't think like that. I must believe she might still be out there. That somehow, she escaped. She's in hiding, waiting for this nightmare to end so she can find me again.

It's a fool's hope, but it's all I have. The only thing keeping me from giving in to the darkness threatening to consume me. A tiny flicker of light in the blackness.

Mama, if you can hear me, please give me a sign. Let me know if you're still with me. I'm trying to be strong, but I need you. I'll never stop needing you. Never stop loving you. Never stop waiting for you to come back to me. Please just do anything to show me you are still with me. Please.

I pace the small room, back and forth, back and forth again. The walls seem to creep in closer with each pass. This place has become my prison.

Alone. The word ricochets through my mind on repeat. A relentless reminder of my isolation. Repeated thoughts over and over play in my mind.

The images flash through my mind on an endless loop - Hamas dragging her away as she screams and struggles. Her cries grow distant. Then silence. I am losing my mind. On some level, I am aware of this. My thoughts are repeating, over, and over, and over.

No. I can't think like that. She might still be out there. Hiding somewhere. I keep waiting for this nightmare to end so she can find me again.

It's foolish hope, but it's all I have left.

The only light pieres the darkness threatening to swallow me. I cling to it desperately.

"Mama, if you can hear my prayers, please give me a sign. Let me know if you're still with me. I'm trying to be strong, but I need you. I'll never stop needing you. Never stop loving you. Never stop waiting for you to come back to me.

Waiting and not knowing is agony. But I must endure. I must believe we'll be together again one day. Until then, I'll keep writing in this diary. Keeping a record of my days without you. Hoping each page brings me closer to the moment I'm back in your arms. Is any of this real? I'm not sure I know anymore."

CHAPTER XVII

I clutch my diary tightly. The walls of this safe room press in on me from all sides. I'm alone. So alone.

I flip through the pages, scanning words that now seem pointless. What good are my scribbled thoughts amid so much chaos and violence? My heart pounds as I imagine the horrors happening above, just beyond the locked door.

I pause on an entry from weeks ago, back when my words flowed freely: "Yael and I played jacks in the yard today. I beat her three games in a row!" Such innocent memories now seem frivolous.

My eyes fill with tears, blurring the words on the page. I slam the diary shut. What meaning can my childish ramblings hold now? I hug my knees to my chest, wishing I could sink into the cold concrete floor and disappear.

The single lightbulb above flickers, buzzing like an insect trapped in a jar.

Shadows dance on the walls. I imagine them as twisted figures, clawing to get inside. To get me.

I squeeze my eyes shut, but I can't block out the muffled screams and explosions from above. I want to melt into my mother's arms, to feel her stroke my hair and tell me everything will be okay. But I don't even know if she's still…

I bite my lip until I taste blood, using the pain to anchor myself in the present. To cling to hope. To salvage my sanity.

I reach again for my diary with quivering fingers. The pen hovers over the page. What words can I possibly write to give meaning to such fear and chaos? I press the tip to the paper, watching an inkblot spread like a Rorschach test.

Maybe my words don't matter. Maybe no one will ever read them. But I must try. For Anne. She wrote even in her darkest moments. I owe it to her to find some flicker of light in all this darkness.

I will write. I will survive this. For them.

I stare at the blank page, waiting for the right words to come. But my mind is a hurricane, swirling with dread and doubt.

What if I never again hear my mother's laughter or see my father's warm smile? What if Yael is out there somewhere, crying and alone?

I imagine the terrorists bursting through the door, their feet crushing my diary underfoot. Dragging me away into the blackness.

My hand trembles as I start to write.

"Dear Anne,

I used to think I was strong. That I could face anything as long as I had my family. But now I feel so small and afraid. This waiting in the dark is endless. How did you do it all those years? Sometimes I want to scream until my voice gives out.

To pound the walls until my fists bleed. Anything to break this torturous silence.

My hope flickers like a guttering candle. I'm terrified it will go out completely, leaving me in cold darkness.

But then I remember you, still writing even when all seemed lost. Your words give me courage, Anne. One day, I hope mine can do the same for someone else.

For now, writing is all I have left. My tether to sanity. I'll keep holding on, if only for one more word, one more line.

Thank you for listening, dear friend. You give me the strength to face another day.

Love,

Rachel"

"Dear Anne,

The minutes drag by. Each tick of the imaginary clock echoes through the empty room. I glance anxiously at the locked door, imagining soldiers bursting in at any moment. My heart pounds. I feel like I'm back in the schoolyard, waiting for the bullies to notice me. Helpless. Exposed.

I wish I could speak to Yael one last time. To hear her infectious laugh and feel her warm hand on mine. She always knew how to make me feel brave, even when I was shaking inside.

What if she's out there right now, calling my name? Running through rubble-filled streets, dodging rockets and gunfire, desperately trying to find me?

Oh Yael, please be safe. Stay hidden. Don't look for me.

Sometimes I still hear my mother's gentle voice, calling me in for dinner. I see my father's smile as he hands me the diary, telling me to write down everything I feel. Everything I see.

'One day, the world will want to know,' he says.

Do they know where ever they are now? Can they sense my fear, even miles away? I hope I've made them proud.

Anne, I'm trying hard to be like you. To find light even in the darkest hour. But waiting and not knowing are so hard. How did you manage?

Still, I will keep writing. For them, for you, and for myself. My words are a lifeline, connecting me to all I hold dear. If I write, I am not alone.

With love and hope,

Rachel"

I clutch my diary tightly, my knuckles aching. The silence in this cramped room is deafening. I long to hear my mother's voice, to feel her arms wrapped around me.

"It's going to be okay, Rachel," she would say. "I'm right here."

But she's not here. No one is. And I don't know if she's even still…

No. I can't think like that. She's alive. She has to be.

I imagine her searching the rubble of our neighborhood, calling my name over and over. I see the fear and desperation in her eyes. She won't stop looking until she finds me.

If only I could tell her that I'm okay, that I'm safe in this hidden room. That her brave, beautiful daughter is alive and waiting for her.

I wish I could see my father's smile just one more time. Hear his deep, reassuring voice telling me not to be afraid. Telling me he loves me, and everything will be alright.

But not knowing is the worst part. My mind spins with terrifying possibilities of what might have happened to them.

Were they able to escape when Hamas came? Did they make it to a shelter in time?

Or are they lying injured somewhere, crying out for help that will never come?

I can't let my thoughts linger there. I must believe we'll be together again. We have to be. This can't be the end.

"Anne, please give me the strength to hold on to hope. Help me find light, even in all this darkness.

I will keep writing, keep waiting, keep believing. One day, we'll all be free.

With wavering faith,

Rachel"

I squeeze my diary tightly, willing the pages to absorb all my fears and doubts. To cleanse my mind of the dark thoughts that creep in.

These two diaries, Anne's and mine are all I have left of my old life. My only companions in this cold, cramped space.

I've poured my heart out onto these pages, trusting that my words will somehow survive. That someone will find this diary after…after I'm gone.

But will it even matter? Will anyone care about the innermost thoughts of a thirteen-year-old girl?

When there is so much loss and suffering in the world, who will stop to read about mine?

I wish I could speak to Anne again. Ask her if she ever doubted herself during those long months in the annex. If her faith in the power of writing ever wavered.

Did she truly believe her diary would one day be read? That her words would echo through history?

Anne was so much stronger than I am. Braver. More hopeful.

While I sat here paralyzed by dread, she found peace in putting pen to paper. She turned her isolation into an opportunity to know herself.

Can I do that? Can I be like Anne?

I must try.

"I need to find the courage to keep writing. If not for myself then for you, Anne.

I promise I won't let fear silence me. I will write to remember all that happened. The people we've lost. The world we used to know.

I will write so that I am not forgotten. So that Rachel Abigail Goldberg will leave some mark on this earth.

Anne, please give me the strength to continue. Be my light when all other lights go out.

With wavering faith,

Rachel"

I stare at the page, my hands trembling. The pen falls from my limp fingers.

My words to Anne stare back at me. Mocking me.

How can I make such promises when I can barely summon the will to lift my pen? Who am I to think my story could inspire anyone?

I'm no Anne Frank. I am just a scared, helpless girl trapped in a nightmare. My words are meaningless scribbles compared to hers.

Tears blur my vision as I stare down at the diary in my lap. The last link to who I used to be. To the girl who still had a family, friends, and a future.

That girl is gone now. There is only this hollow shell sitting alone in the dark.

I should just give up. Stop pretending I have any control over what happens to me. What's the point of writing if no one will ever read it?

My fingers curl around the edges of the diary. I could so easily tear out the pages. Destroy the evidence of my pathetic hopes and delusions.

"No." My whisper echoes against the cold concrete walls.

Anne didn't give up. Even when she was ripped from her home and taken to a death camp, she kept fighting. Kept hoping. Kept dreaming.

I owe it to her to do the same.

With a deep, shuddering breath, I lift the pen again. Press it to the page. The words come slowly at first, then pour out in a torrent.

I write it all down. Every detail. The good and the bad.

When I finally set the pen aside, dawn's light is peeking underneath the doorway. My hand aches, but my heart feels lighter.

Anne was right. Writing is freedom. No matter what happens, I will keep writing.

For you, Anne. Always for you.

I close my eyes and picture Anne huddled in her hidden annex, writing feverishly in her diary. Did she ever imagine her words would be read by millions? That she would become a symbol of hope and resilience for generations to come?

"I'm so sorry, Anne," I whisper. "I'm sorry no one was there to rescue you. To carry you out of that horrible place and bring you somewhere safe."

My voice breaks and tears spill down my cheeks. Why was I spared when she and so many others were not? It's not fair. Anne was so much braver, so much stronger than me. She should have lived to fulfill her dreams, to fall in love, to have a family.

Instead, her life was cut short in the cruelest way. And here I am, still alive when I don't deserve to be. Hidden away while others suffer. I'm nothing but a coward.

"Forgive me," I sob. "Forgive me for being too weak. For not being able to save anyone. Not even myself."

I bury my face in my hands, shoulders shaking with grief for the girl who died alone in Bergen-Belsen. For all the lives that have been lost. For everything that can never be regained. For a holocaust that should have taught the world to never let it happen again.

When the tears finally subside, I lift my head. Wipe my eyes. Pick up the pen once more.

"I'm still here, Anne,"

I write in shaky letters.

"I'm still fighting. Your spirit lives on in me."

It's a promise I intend to keep, no matter what. I will honor Anne's memory to my last breath.

I close the diary. My heart feels as heavy as a stone, but I know I must keep going. I must find the strength to survive another day, and the next.

Anne made it through over two years in hiding with hope and courage. I can make it through this. I must believe that I will see my family again. That we will all be together one day, far away from this nightmare.

Until then, I will write. I'll remember Anne's words, her spirit. She lost everything, but never lost hope. I owe it to her to do the same.

Running my fingers over the worn cover of my diary, I make a silent promise. I will not give up. I will not let fear defeat me. Darkness may surround me, but in my heart, I still have light. Faith. A flicker of hope that refuses to be extinguished.

I am not alone, though it feels that way. Anne walks beside me, urging me on. Her story gives me strength when mine runs out. She will help me make it through this.

Tomorrow I will open my diary again.

I will keep writing, keep hoping, and keep fighting back against the shadows. My words will bear witness, just as Anne's have.

For now, I tuck my diary safely away and lie down on the hard mattress, the only bed I have. Sleep will not come easy, but the light inside me will keep the bad dreams at bay.

I am still alive. Still breathing. And as long as I have that, I have hope.

CHAPTER XVIII

My breath catches in my throat as another explosion rocks the kibbutz. I'm huddled in the corner of the safe room. The distant sounds of gunfire and bombs make my heart hammer inside my ribcage. I squeeze my eyes shut, trying to block it all out.

A sudden scraping noise outside the heavy metal door makes me gasp. My eyes fly open, darting around the small, dark space. Did I imagine it? I hold perfectly still, straining to hear over the thunderous pounding of blood in my ears.

There it is again. Metallic scraping, like something being dragged across the door. I scramble to my feet, palms slick with sweat. Who's out there? Friend or foe? I want to call out, but the words stick in my throat.

The door handle jiggles and then turns with a loud click. I stumble backward, fists clenched, poised for fight or flight. The door swings open, casting a sliver of light into the safe room. A tall silhouette fills the entryway. My heart leaps into my mouth. Is this how I die?

The silhouette steps into the room, features coming into focus in the dim light. It's a teenage boy, tall and lean, with tousled black hair and piercing green eyes. Relief floods through me for a split second before the questions start swirling.

Who is he? How did he get in here? Can I trust him?

He holds up both hands, palms out as if to show he means no harm.

"It's okay," he says, voice low and steady. "I'm here to help you."

I stare at him warily. My mind reels, struggling to make sense of his sudden appearance.

"Who are you?" I demand, proud of the way my voice doesn't shake.

"My name's Ari," he says. "I'm with the resistance."

Resistance? I narrow my eyes. Is this some kind of trap?

He seems to read the suspicion on my face.

"I know you're scared," he says gently. "But you have to trust me, Rachel. I'm getting you out of here."

Hearing my name on this stranger's lips sends a chill down my spine. I take a small step back, shaking my head.

"Why should I trust you?" I challenge, desperate to buy time while I try to gauge just how much danger I'm in. My mind spins scenarios, each more terrifying than the last.

Ari holds my gaze, calm and steady. "Because I'm here to save you," he says simply. Somehow, looking into those solemn green eyes, I feel the first flickers of hope.

I hesitate, searching Ari's face for any sign of deception. But his expression is open and honest. Still, I can't bring myself to let my guard down completely.

"How did you even find me here? How do you know my name?" I ask.

"I've been following the chatter on the internet for weeks now," Ari explains. "I learned about Hamas' plans to attack the kibbutz and came here as soon as I could to get you and others to safety. A neighbor of yours is at a shelter in central Israel and she told me where I would most likely find survivors. See? Here is the list she gave me."

I'm stunned by the risks he must have taken. The courage that must have been required.

"You did all that…for me?" I whisper.

Ari gives a single nod. "For you and your people. My family lost many in the holocaust. I can't let this happen again."

My heart swells, even as my mind rebels against fully trusting this virtual stranger. But what choice do I have?

Ari glances toward the door, face grim. "We have to move quickly. It won't be long before they find this place."

Fear lances through me. We're running out of time. I take a
deep breath and make my decision.

"Okay," I say. "I'm with you."

Ari's eyes light up. He reaches for my hand.

"Let's go."

I hesitate for a moment, my hand hovering uncertainly over
his outstretched one. Can I really trust him? He seems so
sincere, but I know nothing about him. What if this is some
kind of trap?

My eyes dart around the cramped space of the safe room,
taking in the bare walls, and the piles of musty blankets. It's
not much of a refuge. Gunfire crackles faintly outside.

I think of my brother, my parents, my friends. Are they out
there somewhere, fighting for their lives? While I cower in
here, useless?

Ari is watching me patiently, hand still extended. His eyes are full of compassion.

"I know you're scared," he says gently. "But we can get through this together. I give you my word, Rachel—I will protect you."

A lump forms in my throat. When was the last time someone looked at me with such care and concern?

Slowly, I placed my hand in his. His fingers curl around mine, warm and reassuring. For the first time since this nightmare started, I feel a tiny spark of hope.

"Let's go," I whisper.

Ari gives my hand a squeeze. Moving swiftly, he shoulders his rifle and turns toward the door. After a brief pause, he eases it open, just a crack. Peering out cautiously.

My heart hammers against my ribs. This is it. No turning back now.

With a deep breath, I hoist my backpack with the two diaries on my back and I follow Ari out into the smoky twilight. Toward an uncertain future.

We slip out into the hazy dusk, the air thick with smoke and ash. I stay close behind Ari as we creep alongside the safe room, pressing our bodies against the crumbling wall.

He pauses, peering around the corner toward the main building. Then he turns back to me, voice barely above a whisper.

"First we need to make our way across the courtyard. There's a lot of open ground, so we'll have to stay low and move quickly."

I nod, wide-eyed.

"Once we reach the east wing, there's a hidden tunnel that will take us under the kibbutz perimeter fence." He points toward a copse of trees in the distance. "Our best chance is to use the forest as cover. If we can make it to the ravine, we can regroup and catch our breath."

It sounds terrifying. Dangerous. But the determination in Ari's eyes helps steady my nerves.

"I'll follow your lead," I tell him.

He gives my hand another reassuring squeeze. Then we're off, sprinting across the open courtyard. I run faster than I've ever run before, my lungs burning.

Just a little further. We're going to make it.

We dart from building to building, staying low to the ground. My heart pounds in my ears as we pause behind a crumbling wall at the edge of the tree line to catch our breath.

I glance at Ari. His jaw is set, eyes scanning our surroundings. He seems so brave, so focused. I wish I could be that fearless.

"The tunnel entrance is just ahead," he whispers.

I peer around the edge of the wall. A small metal hatch is nestled at the base of the east wing, nearly invisible unless you know where to look.

We move toward it quickly, crouching down. Ari pulls at the hatch - it creaks open reluctantly, just wide enough for us to slip through. The dank tunnel looms before us.

He looks at me, brows furrowed. "Stay right behind me, okay? It will be completely dark soon."

I nod, willing my voice not to shake. "Okay."

With a deep breath, I follow Ari into the inky blackness. He pulls the hatch closed behind us. I blink rapidly, trying to adjust to the sudden darkness. The only sound is our shallow breathing and the scuff of shoes on the dirt floor.

We make our way through the narrow passage cautiously. I focus on the faint outline of Ari's shoulders just ahead, trusting him to lead us to safety.

Minutes drag by. Just when I feel I can't take the oppressive darkness any longer, Ari slows. "We're almost there," he murmurs. "Get ready to run."

I grip the straps of my backpack tightly, diaries tucked safely inside, as the tunnel begins to brighten. We must be nearing the exit.

My legs burn with anticipation, ready to run but forced to creep along in the confines of the passageway. I try to prepare myself for what's coming next. Will I even have the strength for it? I have not had proper nourishment or exercise in such a very long time.

The hatch at the end is sealed shut. Ari strains to open it just enough for us to slip through. A sliver of hazy light spills in, revealing a bombed-out street.

"On three," Ari says. "One, two..."

Before he can finish, an explosion rocks the ground, throwing both of us off balance. My heart leaps into my throat. They've found us.

"Go, go!" Ari yells.

We burst out of the tunnel into chaos. The air is choked with smoke and dust. Gunfire bursts out nearby. I run blindly, my only thought to get as far away as I can.

Somehow Ari keeps pace, guiding me down the side streets and through decimated buildings. We just need to make it to the checkpoint, though it feels impossibly far now.

I push myself harder despite the burning in my lungs. We're so close. I can't give up after coming this far. Ari's voice echoes in my mind: "Just a little farther..." I wonder just for a moment if I should have stayed in my little room.

CHAPTER XIX

The sunlight filters through the slats of the boarded windows, casting bars of light across Ari's face. He sleeps soundly, his chest rising and falling in a steady rhythm. I watch him for a moment, struck by how peaceful he looks. Hard to believe this is the same boy who stared down the barrel of a rifle just yesterday without flinching.

My hands tremble as I recall the moment - Ari boldly standing his ground as I cowered hidden in the shadows. He didn't hesitate, even with the barrel aimed square at his forehead. Just kept his gaze fixed and his voice steady until the thief backed down. I don't know where he found such courage.

I glance down at my diary, trailing my fingers over the worn cover. Ari's bravery has inspired me. Giving me a sense of hope I thought was lost. If he can be so fearless, perhaps I can too.

I flip through the pages, each word a testament to our struggle. My words. If I can tell our story, and keep our memories alive, maybe I can make a difference too.

The pencil that I found in the street hovers over the paper. My hand steadies. I begin to write.

I let the pencil glide across the page, describing Ari's act of courage in vivid detail. The thief's snarling threats, the glint of the rifle barrel, the bead of sweat trailing down Ari's temple - I capture it all. I want anyone who reads this to truly understand what bravery looks like.

My writing flows easily, faster than it has in weeks. Ari's example has lit a fire within me. I feel focused and determined. My pencil scratches furiously, trying to keep up with my thoughts.

I pause, glancing again at Ari's sleeping form. He looks so peaceful, so innocent. Hard to believe he has such bravery within him. But I've seen it again and again - his refusal to show fear, his willingness to take risks to help others. He inspires me to be stronger.

I turn back to my diary, mouth set in a determined line. If Ari can be brave, so can I. These pages are my act of courage, my way to make a difference. I will tell our story with honesty, capturing both the beautiful and the ugly.

Bear witness so others know we existed, we fought, we mattered.

My hand trembles slightly as I write the next lines.

"I am still afraid, still uncertain of our fate. But when I glance at Ari, I feel hope. His bravery reminds me that even in darkness, light can shine through. As long as we keep fighting, and keep holding onto hope, we have a chance. I will continue writing, for him, for us, for the future."

My pencil moves steadily on, word by word, line by line. Our story continues.

I nod to myself, my resolve hardening. This diary is important - it deserves to be written. To be remembered.

Our lives hang by a thread each day. Death looms, bleak and heavy. It would be so easy to give up and surrender to despair.

But that's not who we are. We cling to life desperately, savoring each breath, and each moment with loved ones. Even now, huddled in this abandoned, bombed-out building, we have laughter, tears, memories.

My pencil presses harder against the page. Our stories can't disappear into the darkness, lost forever when we are gone. Through these pages, we will live on. Be remembered. I will capture our fear and our pain, but also our hope, our love, and our unrelenting will to survive.

Future generations may read this diary. What will they learn from our struggle? Will it inspire them, and give them courage? The thought makes my heart beat faster. I may be just a girl, but my words could resonate through the years, lighting a flame in others, like Anne's did.

I glance at Ari again, drawing strength from his sleeping form. Because of his bravery, I found my own. My pencil is a weapon, my diary a shield. I will write our truth, come what may.

I nod, a renewed sense of purpose flowing through me. My pencil scratches furiously, racing to keep up with my thoughts.

"These pages hold power - I see that now. Though we face darkness, my words will shine light for those who come after. They will know we did not go gently, but fought for every breath, every day. Our voices will echo even when we are gone."

I think of my hero Anne Frank, who wrote her diary alone in that attic long ago. She spoke truth in a time of lies and kept hope alive during hopeless times. Without her words, how much would we have lost?

My diary may seem small, or insignificant. But words spread like wildfire, igniting change. Thoughts become actions, one heart touching another until a firestorm blazes through the apathy. I want my words to burn bright, searing truth into this unjust world.

There is so much I still fear. Death prowls, biding its time. Each day could be our last. But I will stare down that darkness and write anyway. For my people, my future, my own soul - I must.

I glance again at Ari, drawing courage from his sleeping form. My dear friend, you showed me the power of bravery. Because of you, I found my voice. It is small, but it will not be silenced.

My pencil continues its dance across the page. Words pour from my heart. I write fiercely, defiantly - determined to tell our story, come what may.

I take a deep, shaky breath, trying to steady my nerves. The fear is always with me, coiled tight in my chest. It whispers that we cannot win, that all is already lost.

But then I look at my diary, open in my lap. The pages are filled with our struggles, our small victories, our flickering hopes. This book is the chronicle of our fight. It proves we persevered, day after day when all seemed darkest.

My pencil moves slowly at first, then gains momentum. I will describe the tiny safe room and the bread we shared for dinner. Tiny details are monumental to me. I etch them into history.

I write about Ari's unwavering spirit. The light in his eyes that not even war could extinguish. His resilience fuels my own. As long as we have breath, we have hope.

The mantra transports me, weaving a bridge from this building to some far-off place and time. Decades from now, perhaps someone will read my story. Will they feel what I feel? Will they be able to understand? If my diary can shine a light on even one soul, it will have served its purpose.

I write as if my life depended on it. In some ways, it does. These pages tether me to hope, to meaning. They remind me I am not alone, though sometimes it feels like I am.

My pencil continues scratching, bearing witness. I write, and write, determined to leave a mark on this world. My small voice joins a mighty chorus - the defiant shouts of all who fight persecution and oppression. Though darkness threatens, hope flickers on. Together, we light the way.

I take a deep breath and let my pencil guide me.

"Dear Anne,

Today I find myself grateful. Not for the moldy bread or bombed-out building. But for Ari. His courage lifts my spirits when they are low. He reminds me that even in darkness, stars find a way to shine.

Without Ari, I would be lost. His bravery pushes me to be brave too. He does not accept defeat, so neither can I. When he smiles at me from across the room, I feel less alone.

I wish I could be more like him. Fear still flickers inside me. But Ari's light keeps it at bay. He gives me the strength to lift my pencil each day. To leave my mark through words, as he does through deeds.

We have only each other now. But with Ari by my side, I feel I can face anything. Even the darkest night must yield to dawn eventually. When the sun rises, we will rise with it.

Until then, I will write. I will tell our story to anyone who will listen. I will shout into the darkness until my voice gives out. Then I will whisper. But I will never stop.

If we do not make it out of this nightmare, I hope somehow my diary does. May my words offer comfort to those who feel alone and afraid, as I do now. Together, we can kindle the light again.

With eternal hope,

Rachel"

I put down my pencil and close the diary. Ari smiles at me from across the room, his eyes full of warmth. When we have each other, there is light.

CHAPTER XX

The dim light of the oil lamp barely illuminates the pages in my diary. We huddle together in the dank tunnel, the air heavy with tension. Ari's face is etched with grim determination, one hand resting on the rifle slung across his chest. He stands rigid, barking orders to the others. His voice echoes off the concrete walls.

I can barely breathe. Not knowing - will we make it out alive? - claws at my insides. I force my pen across the page.

Ari shifts, boots scraping the floor. Someone coughs. The shuffle of nervous feet vibrates through me.

My thoughts race. How did we get here? Weeks ago, we were safe. Now our home is destroyed, and our friends and family are torn apart. We flee like rats through these tunnels, hunted at every turn.

My hands shake so much I can barely form the letters. But I must record this. Bear witness. If I don't, who will?

Ari checks his watch, face etched in stone. "It's time. Let's move."

Rifles cock, bags rustle. We look at each other, wanting to memorize each face. Just in case.

I snap my diary shut and slip it into my bag. I look back once more at the place that sheltered us and kept us alive this long. One haven among many scattered throughout the wreckage.

Ari squeezes my shoulder. "Stay close." I force a nod, blinking back weary tears.

We plunge into the dark unknown. Again.

I take a deep breath as we stumble into the night. The air is acrid, burning my throat. In the distance, a red glow sears the sky. The sounds of gunfire and explosions make my heart thunder.

I glance at Ari.

His jaw is tight, eyes scanning our surroundings. I want to melt into him, let his strength wrap around me like a shield.

We creep along in a single file behind him. He pauses at corners, raising a clenched fist before waving us onward. I grasp the straps of my bookbag, knuckles white.

As we skirt the remains of a building, the rubble shifts under my feet. I freeze, holding my breath. The others pause, rifles aimed into the darkness.

Ari shakes his head, and we continue. Still, my nerves jangle with each step.

We come upon a collapsed section of wall blocking our path. Ari mutters under his breath. We backtrack and slip down a narrow alley, the blackness swallowing us.

I want to beg them to slow down, to let me catch my breath. But their urgent pace brooks no argument. I force my trembling legs onward.

Somewhere close by, a burst of gunfire shatters the night. I clench my teeth to hold back a scream. Breathe, I tell myself. Just breathe.

We are the hunted, scurrying for our lives. Like rats in a sewer. But we will not cower or give in. Together, we will survive this nightmare. My pencil scratches furiously, every chance I get, determined to tell our story.

We emerge from the alley into a courtyard strewn with rubble and debris. I stumble over a chunk of concrete, scraping my hand. Ari grabs my arm, steadying me. His touch is a lifeline, keeping me grounded amidst the chaos.

Moonlight cuts through the haze, illuminating the skeletal remains of buildings. Somewhere in the distance, a thin plume of smoke coils into the sky. The metallic tang of ash coats my tongue.

I want to block it all out and pretend this isn't real. That any moment I'll wake up safe in my bed. But the truth is etched into the landscape—the broken streets, the hollow structures. This is our reality now.

We pick our way across the courtyard, glass, and metal shards crunching under our feet. I cling to the shadows, praying we remain unseen. A dog howls mournfully, then falls silent.

Ari's hushed voice drifts back. "Stay sharp. We're close now."

Close to what? Safety? Refuge? I hardly dare to hope. But I grip my diary tighter, trusting in the promise of his words. We will make it through this. We must.

Step by step, breath by breath, we will survive. My pencil continues its whispered rebellion, bearing witness until the bitter end. I want to know about my family, but I can't think about them now. Everyone is hyper-focused on pure survival. We are the hunted.

Ari's grip on my arm tightens as we reach the far side of the courtyard. I glance at him, reading the tension in his furrowed brow. His eyes dart left and right, scanning for threats.

"Get down," he hisses suddenly, pushing me behind a pile of debris. I crouch low, my heart hammering against my ribs.

In the distance, harsh voices cut through the night. Ari presses a finger to his lips, signaling silence. The voices draw nearer, accompanied by the crunch of boots on gravel. A beam from a flashlight skitters across the rubble, missing us by inches.

I squeeze my eyes shut, willing myself to melt into the shadows. Beside me, Ari's breathing is shallow, his body coiled tight as a spring. I can feel his desperation to keep us hidden radiating in waves.

After what feels like an eternity, the voices fade into the distance. Ari sags in relief, his forehead dropping briefly to touch mine. "That was close," he murmurs.

Too close. The knife-edge we walk has never felt sharper. How long can we evade them before our luck runs out? I don't want to find out.

Ari helps me to my feet. We hurry to catch up with the others, who have reached the next alley. Racing against time, racing towards an uncertain future. But as long as we're together, I can keep putting one foot in front of the other.

We press on through the ravaged streets, the rubble slowing our progress. My legs burn with exertion as I clamber over piles of broken concrete and twisted metal. I trip, skinning my knee on the jagged remains of a brick wall. The pain is sharp but fleeting. There's no time to stop and tend to small wounds.

I glance back at the others. Faces etched with grim determination, shoulders sagging under the weight of hasty packs. Others like me that we have rescued along the way. How much farther can we push ourselves physically? Our supplies are minimal, and the landscape itself seems determined to thwart us. Our little ragtag group of two has turned into almost a dozen now.

Another blocked passage. Ari scans the route ahead, brow furrowed. "This way," he says finally, pointing towards a narrow gap between two buildings. I shudder, imagining us trapped if the structures collapse. But we have no choice except to trust Ari's judgment.

Single file, we edge into the tight space. My torn knee stings as it scrapes the rough wall. I feel claustrophobic, hemmed in on all sides. But I force myself to keep putting one foot in front of the other. Eyes fixed ahead on Ari's back, willing us towards safety.

At last, we emerge, the path opening before us. I let out a shaky breath. We're still in one piece. Still moving forward. That's all that matters now. Surviving to see the next minute, the next hour. Time is measured in small victories of steps taken, and obstacles overcome.

I sink down against a crumbled wall, finally allowing my exhausted body a moment's rest. The others slump beside me, gulping water, and massaging cramped muscles. No words pass between us. Our focus narrows to taking in air, willing our hearts to slow. There is no energy wasted on words.

In the distance, the sounds of warfare continue unabated. Gunfire. Explosions. Screams. The never-ending soundtrack of the last weeks. I close my eyes, unsuccessfully blocking it out.

Ari stands watch, peering around the corner into the alley ahead. I study his face, stern and unflinching. Have the horrors we've witnessed penetrated that military-hardened exterior? What inner turmoil boils beneath the surface?

"Five more minutes," he says. "Then we have to move."

I nod, knowing too well the fragility of our refuge. Safety is measured only in moments, while danger lurks around every turn.

Ari offers me some dried fruit from his pack. I take it gratefully, my empty stomach clenching. When was my last real meal? The days blur together now.

But the fruit fills my mouth with sweetness. Its taste, like this rest, is a small respite to cherish. Tiny rays of light in the darkness. They give me the strength to continue this grueling journey.

I will endure this. We will endure. Stumbling blindly through the ruins, propelled only by stubborn will. Because we must. Because the alternative is unthinkable. And so, we press on, one aching step after another. Towards what, we no longer know. Only away, always away from here.

Ari motions us forward, and we emerge cautiously from the alley. My muscles protest, exhausted. I yearn to stop, to rest, but we must move.

I stay close behind Ari as we creep down debris-strewn streets. He pauses at every intersection, gun ready, before signaling us onward. My eyes dart around wildly, alert for any sign of danger. But the bombed-out buildings stand silent, their gaping windows like the eyes of the dead, staring.

We slog through the rubble, squeezing through cracks and holes smashed in walls. The air hangs heavy with dust, grit coating my throat with each breath. Sweat plasters my hair to my skin.

How much farther can we go on like this? Then I see it up ahead. A door, hanging crookedly. The shelter.

My pace quickens.

Sanctuary lies so close. Ari reaches the small shelter first, yanking open the door, gun lifted. He scans the interior, then waves us inside.

We hurry in, and Ari slams the door shut. For the first time in days, the sounds of war are muffled. Here, we are cocooned. Hidden. Safe.

My body sags, the adrenaline rush fading. I sink down against the wall. Around me, the others do the same. No words, just heavy breathing. We made it.

Then I smelled it. Warm, yeasty. Bread. My eyes widen, and I see a pot bubbling over a small fire. After so much hunger, my stomach growls at this feast.

I don't care what tomorrow brings. For now, we rest. We survive. We eat.

I tear into the bread ravenously, not even caring that it burns my tongue. No meal has ever tasted so good. The knots in my stomach finally begin to unwind.

Ari passes around a jug of water.

I gulp it down, the cool liquid soothing my raw throat. For these precious moments, I can forget about everything happening outside these walls.

But the images are seared into my mind. The bombs falling. Buildings crumbling. Bodies in the streets. Women, children, babies, the elderly. I squeeze my eyes shut, trying to block it out.

No, I cannot forget. I must remember so that others know our story. Know the horrors we endured. The struggles we overcame.

I take out my diary, its pages now wrinkled and torn. But the words inside are still intact. My account of life in the ghost town our kibbutz has become.

I will keep writing. Keep recording. One day, these pages will be found. One day, our voices will be heard. Our lives mattered.

For now, we have each other. We have hope. Tomorrow, we will rise and continue our journey. But tonight, we rest. We go on.

CHAPTER XXI

The acrid smell of smoke burns my nose. I grip Ari's hand tightly as we creep through the rubble far from the perimeter of our kibbutz. My eyes dart around, searching for any sign of the enemy. The eerie silence weighs heavy. Each crunch of our footsteps on shattered glass makes me wince. I want to scream just to break it.

"Almost there," Ari whispers. His voice is steady but his fingers tremble in mine.

I nod, afraid to make a sound. We hurdled over a crumbling wall. Our ragtag group follows suit. My foot catches on a chunk of concrete and I stumble. Ari's grip on my hand stops me from falling. I bite my lip to keep from crying out.

"You okay?" His eyes are full of concern.

I force a tight smile and blink back tears. "I'm fine."

We press on through the destruction — our homeland, reduced to wreckage. I don't recognize the streets anymore.

My heart pounds against my ribs. I just want to get to
somewhere safe.

In the distance, I spot the shelter door. Ari sees it too. We
break into a run. The promise of refuge pushes us forward.
Almost there. Just a little further…

We reach the heavy metal door and Ari pulls it open with a
grunt. A sliver of light spills out and we hurry inside. Ari
slams the door shut behind us and spins the wheel to lock it.

My eyes take a moment to adjust to the dim lighting. It's
cooler here, and my lungs fill with dank but breathable air.
The shelter is bare - just a few cots, some boxes of supplies,
a radio, and a kerosene lamp hanging from the ceiling.

But we made it. Against all odds, we're here.

My knees go weak, and I sink down onto one of the cots.
The thin mattress squeaks under my weight. I bury my face
in my hands as a sob escapes my throat.

Ari's footsteps approach and then his arms wrap around me.

I cling to him and let the tears fall. We stay like that for a long time, holding each other in the near darkness.

"It's going to be okay, Rachel," Ari murmurs into my hair. "We're safe now. It's over for now."

I nod against his chest, trying to believe it. But the images of my destroyed home haunt me. The horrors we've seen can't be unseen.

Ari's steady heartbeat and the feeling of his fingers combing through my hair eventually calm me. I take a shaky breath and sit up. Ari's green eyes search mine.

"We made it," I whisper.

Ari nods, his jaw set with determination. "We're survivors."

I wipe my eyes and look around the shelter again. It's sparse, but we have the essentials. Food, water, shelter. We can rest here. Regroup. Figure out what comes next.

My gaze settles on the radio. I stand up and shuffle over to it, turning the knobs. Static hisses from the speakers.

"Do you think we can get any news on that thing?" I asked Ari.

He comes over and fiddles with the dials. More static. Then a faint voice cuts through. I grasp Ari's arm as we strain to listen.

"…Hamas decimated…only small pockets remain…evacuation routes established…"

The signal fades in and out, but we hear enough. A cautious spark of hope ignites in my chest.

"It might be over soon," Ari says.

I nod, my mind racing. "Do you think they've heard anything about our families? My Mama and Papa?" My voice catches.

Ari squeezes my hand. "We'll find them, Rachel. I promise."

I close my eyes, picturing my parents' faces, willing them to be okay. We listen to the radio static, clinging to the bits of news that offer a lifeline. The war rages on above, but down here in the shelter, we have a moment of peace.

I take a deep breath, trying to calm my racing thoughts. The news from the radio echoes in my mind - Hamas decimated, evacuation routes. Could this nightmare finally be ending?

My eyes drift around the sparse shelter. Just four concrete walls, a few cots, and some basic supplies. But it's enough for now. Enough to rest and regroup before we move forward.

I glance at Ari. His brow is furrowed as he continues fiddling with the radio dial. Static hisses and pops, interspersed with faint voices speaking words I strain to understand. My heart leaps every time a full sentence comes through clearly.

"…peace negotiations underway…"

"...international forces to deploy as peacekeepers..."

With each snippet, the spark inside me glows brighter.
After endless days of destruction and loss, hope feels
foreign. But it's there. Dim, but growing.

I sink onto a cot, suddenly exhausted. Ari looks over,
concern in his eyes. "Get some rest, Rachel. I'll keep
watch."

I nod, laying back and closing my eyes. The hard cot
provides little comfort, but sleep comes quickly anyway.
My dreams are filled with visions of reuniting with my
family. Of walking outside without fear. Of peace.

I'm jolted awake by a melodic chirping. For a moment, I'm
disoriented. The gentle birdsong feels out of place amidst
the harsh sounds of war.

As wakefulness returns, the events of the last few days come
flooding back. The rescue. The evacuation. We made it out.

My legs wobble as I stand, weak after so long in the safe room and then days in the shelter. I shuffle towards the open door, hunger and curiosity overcoming caution.

The sun's warmth on my face is soothing. My eyes drift shut, and I turn my face upwards, embracing the light. A breeze ruffles my hair, carrying the scent of wildflowers.

The birds continue their cheerful song. I open my eyes, spotting a pair flitting between the trees nearby. Their small forms seem impossibly delicate after witnessing so much destruction.

Yet still they sing. Still, there is beauty to be found.

I take a deep breath, filling my lungs with fresh air. The knot in my chest loosens slightly. There is hope ahead. If we can survive the darkest days, we can survive what comes next.

One step at a time, we will make it through.

I tear my gaze away from the birds.

I take in my surroundings. There are others here - survivors
like me. Some sit alone, staring blankly ahead. Others
gather in small groups, speaking in hushed voices. Some are
clearly wounded. Most have wounds that we will never see.

All bear the same haunted look in their eyes that I'm sure is
mirrored in my own. We have endured the unendurable
together.

One figure stands out from the rest. Ari. His tall frame is
silhouetted against the morning sun. As if sensing my gaze,
he turns.

Our eyes meet. In his emerald, green irises, I see my own
bone-deep exhaustion reflected back at me. But I see
strength there too. Determination. We have so much left to
do, but we will face it together.

After a long moment, he holds out his hand. I go to him,
twining my fingers with his. No words are needed. The
battle may be over, but the war rages on in our hearts.

Yet with Ari by my side, I feel I can weather any storm
ahead.

The road will be long, but we will walk it hand in hand. Where he leads, I will follow.

I cling to Ari's hand like a lifeline, the warmth and solidity of his palm pressed against mine grounding me in this moment. So much has changed in such a short span of time. The world I knew is gone, shattered like glass under the destructive force of war. I feel like a refugee in my own skin, unsure of how to navigate this new reality.

My mind flashes back to the cramped confines of the shelter, the wailing of the air raid sirens, the choking grip of fear as the bombs fell all around us. I remember Ari's arms encircling me, his quiet strength and reassurance as we huddled together. We endured the worst humanity had to offer and emerged on the other side, forever altered.

Now, standing in this oasis of relative safety, I almost don't recognize myself. The girl who skipped to school each morning clutching her books, who stayed up late reading novels by flashlight - that innocent soul is no more. In her place is someone older, wearier, stripped of naivety. My heart aches for all that has been lost.

But as I meet Ari's eyes again, I see understanding there.

We have weathered the same storms and fought the same battles. Together we have survived against impossible odds. Though the world may never be the same, there is hope to be found in the simplest of human connections.

I give Ari's hand a grateful squeeze, taking comfort in its solid warmth. When we stand united, I know I can face whatever comes next. War has taken so much, but it has not taken everything.

I take a deep breath, filling my lungs with clean, fresh air. No more acrid smell of smoke, no more lingering scent of fear. Just oxygen, pure and sweet.

My legs are unsteady beneath me, trembling with disuse after being confined for so long. But I force them to carry me forward, one small step at a time. The sun's rays warm my skin, the light almost too bright after days spent inside and underground. I raise my hand to shield my eyes as I scan our surroundings.

Other refugees mill about, their faces etched with the same bone-deep weariness I feel. We are all survivors here. Battle-hardened, weary, but still standing. Still breathing.

I spot a woman handing out bottles of water and make my way toward her, throat parched. The cool liquid soothes me as it flows down, reviving me. I save a few sips for Ari, watching his shoulders relax as he drinks.

Now that our basic needs are met, my thoughts turn to my family. Have they made it to safety too? Or are they…? I can't complete the thought. I must believe they also found refuge, just as Ari and I did.

I know there are aid workers here, people who can help reconnect loved ones torn apart by war. My next step is clear - I must find them. With Ari's hand clasped in mine, I steel myself and walk onward. Not knowing is a constant ache, but soon I will have answers. Come what may, we will face it together.

CHAPTER XXII

Blinking. I'm blinking into sunlight so bright it makes my eyes ache. How long was I in that cramped, windowless safe room? Days? Weeks? Time lost meaning down there in the dark. Now I'm standing in the rubble, the devastation stretching as far as I can see. Twisted metal and shattered concrete surround me. The air is thick with smoke and dust, burning my throat with each breath. But there is sunshine.

My body feels like one big bruise. Each movement sends pain shooting through my exhausted muscles. Cuts crisscross my arms and legs, stinging reminders of my escape from the collapsed building. Blood and grime coat my skin. I want to lay down right here among the debris. Give in to the bone-deep weariness that's threatening to pull me under.

But I force my leaden legs to take another step. Then another. I must find my family. My friends. Are they even still alive? I must believe they made it to safety like I did. They must be here somewhere amidst the chaos. I just need to keep looking.

So, I walk on, scanning the devastation for any familiar face.

My heart pounds out a frantic rhythm, fueled by fear and desperate hope. Where are they? Are they hurt? Are they even alive? Each second that ticks by without answers feels like an eternity. I want to scream out their names, but my raw throat can only manage a hoarse croak.

Come on, let me find them. I can't do this alone. Please, just one glimpse of someone I know. One sign that I'm not totally alone in this hellscape. I don't know how much more I can take. But I force myself to keep walking. Keep searching. Because giving up is not an option. Not yet.

I'm about to give up hope when suddenly I see her. Esther, one of my friends since we were little kids. She's sitting against the remains of a concrete wall, blankly staring into the distance. Before I even think, I'm sprinting towards her.

"Esther!" My voice comes out in a sobbing gasp.

She turns, and for a split-second confusion clouds her eyes. Then recognition lights up her face.

"Rachel!"

We crashed into each other, both weeping with relief. I cling to her like I'll never let go, feeling her solid warmth against me. She's real. She's alive.

When we finally pull apart, there are tears streaming down both our faces. I grasp her hands tightly, reassuring myself that this is not a dream.

"You made it," I whisper.

She nods, fresh tears spilling down her cheeks. "We were so scared, Rachel. I thought..." Her voice trails off as a sob escapes her.

"Me too," I say softly. "But we're together now. We're alive."

At that moment, I see other familiar faces emerging from the ruins behind Esther. My neighbors, my friends. More tears fall as I take in each precious, beautiful face. They're battered and shell-shocked, but here. Against all odds, we've found each other again.

I turn back to Esther, managing a shaky smile. "We're going to be okay," I told her, feeling that truth resonate through me for the first time. As long as we have each other, we can make it through this.

I take a deep breath, trying to steady myself. My legs feel unsteady, my hands trembling. The air is thick with smoke and dust, burning my throat with each breath. I blink against the harsh sunlight, taking in the devastation surrounding me.

The kibbutz is barely recognizable. Buildings that once stood tall now lie in shattered ruins. Scattered debris litters the ground - broken glass, twisted metal, chunks of concrete. The earth is scorched black in places, trees are reduced to charred skeletons. It looks like the apocalypse came through here. But the horror of the bodies that I waded through when Ari and I fled, those are gone. They will forever live on in my memory, but the streets are as if they were never there. Erased from history.

My gaze lands on a familiar building, now just a pile of rubble. I feel my heart clench. That used to be the library, where I spent so many peaceful afternoons reading and dreaming. Now it's gone, just like so much else.

I tear my eyes away, not wanting to see the cruel extent of the destruction. But I can't block it out. There, the community hall where we held celebrations. Over there, the dining hall where we shared meals. All destroyed.

But buildings can be rebuilt. What truly hurts is picturing the lives lost here. Friends, family, neighbors. I don't know how many made it and how many didn't. I'm almost afraid to find out.

A gentle hand on my shoulder pulls me from my thoughts. I turn to see Esther looking at me, her eyes full of understanding.

"We will get through this," she says firmly.

I nod, managing a small smile. With my friend by my side, it is easier to face whatever comes next. I repeatedly keep reminding myself of this. There are so many that have far less.

I take a deep breath and start walking through the rubble with Esther. All around us, others are emerging from shelters and bombed-out buildings. I see shock, grief, and exhaustion on their faces. But also resolve. We have survived, and now we must carry on.

I scan the crowd anxiously, looking for my family. And then I see them - my parents, my brother. I let out a sob and ran to them, throwing my arms around them. We cling to each other, crying with relief.

"Thank God you're alright," my mother whispers, stroking my hair. Even in this nightmare, with one brother gone, I have been blessed. Not everyone was so lucky.

As we break apart, I see a familiar figure approaching. It's Mr. Cohen, our neighbor. But his usual warm smile is gone, replaced by a look of bottomless sorrow. I know before he even speaks.

"Yael didn't make it," he choked out. "A shell hit our shelter."

Yael. My best friend. We grew up together. Played together, dreamed together. My heart breaks for her, for the future she will never have. I begin to cry again, this time in grief.

Mr. Cohen embraces me. "She loved you so much," he murmurs. "We will honor her memory."

All around us, the scenes repeat. Families reunite, and others learn their loved ones are gone. We mourn together, drawing strength from one another. In our shared loss, we are bonded closer than ever.

Out of tragedy, compassion appears. Someone passes out food and water. A doctor tends to the wounded. People reach out to comfort strangers. No matter what, we will carry on.

I wander through the shattered kibbutz, numb. The familiar buildings are broken, scarred by bullets and explosions. Remnants of our peaceful life together lie scattered in the dirt - a child's toy, a shattered picture frame. It is almost unrecognizable now.

My limbs feel heavy, and my body and spirit are drained. But I know I cannot stop moving. There are still people who need help. I spot a little girl, no older than five, standing alone and crying. I go to her and bend down.

"Hi sweetie, I'm Rachel. What's your name?" I ask gently.

"Sarah," she sniffles.

"Where are your parents, Sarah?"

"I can't find them!" she wails. "I want my mommy!"

My heart aches for her. I take her small hand in mine. "It's going to be okay. I'll stay with you until we find them."

Sarah throws her arms around me, sobbing into my shoulder. I rub her back soothingly like my mother used to do for me. In this simple act of comforting a child, I find purpose again. My inner light glows brighter, pushing back the darkness.

When Sarah finally calms down, I stand and lift her into my arms.

She is so light, so fragile. But young children are also resilient. They give me hope. My childhood seems like it was ages ago.

I carry her towards the makeshift medical station, glancing down at her as she rests her head against my chest. Her eyelids droop in exhaustion.

"You're safe now," I murmur.

My diary is calling to me, needing me to write down these moments. I must record the pain, but also the love. For one day, I hope, my words will inspire others. Like Anne Frank inspired me. Her spirit is with me, guiding me even now. I can feel it.

I nod off even as I walk, nearly stumbling over scattered debris. My eyelids feel heavy, and my body and mind are utterly spent. But I force myself to continue placing one foot in front of the other.

I focus on the weight of Sarah's small body in my arms, her warmth pressing against me. She breathes softly, already asleep. How I envy the innocence of children, and their ability to find rest even amidst chaos.

My heart aches for those who didn't make it. Friends, family, strangers. Why was I spared when so many others were not? Survivor's guilt weighs upon my soul.

I think of my friend's kind eyes, now forever closed. My spirited baby brother, his laughter silenced. Neighbors and classmates, their dreams unfulfilled. They deserved life as much as I did. More than I did.

"I'm so sorry," I whisper into the smoke-filled air. "I wish I could have saved you too."

Tears slip down my cheeks. I swallow back sobs so as not to wake Sarah. My steps feel heavier now, burdened with grief.

But I must keep going. I cannot let the light inside me be extinguished. I must honor those who passed by embracing life fully, just as Anne Frank did for so long in that dark attic. She is my inspiration still.

When we reached the medical station, I found Sarah's parents sobbing in relief. As they embrace their daughter, joy chases away some of the sorrow in my heart. I did this small thing. I helped reunite a family.

Anne showed me that even the smallest acts of courage and kindness matter. Her spirit gave me strength when I felt lost. Because of her, I will keep writing, keep hoping, and keep living. Her voice within me whispers gently: go on.

CHAPTER XXIII

The crunch of broken glass under my shoes is the first sound that punctures the heavy silence as our family steps cautiously through the rubble-strewn streets, nearing closer to what was our home. My eyes sweep over the devastation - buildings reduced to hollow shells, jagged shards of glass littering the sidewalks, remnants of lives shattered and blown apart.

This was our home.

I clutch my mother's hand tightly, the need for comfort and reassurance coursing through me. My heart pounds against my ribs as we pick our way forward, the air still thick with dust and smoke. It's like walking through the aftermath of a violent earthquake - so much destruction in the wake of the bombs.

"Be careful," my father says, his voice low and tense. He scans the crumbling structures around us, wary of instability and falling debris. I wonder if our house is still standing.

My brother trails behind silently, face pale beneath the dirt and grime. His hand rests on the knife at his belt, knuckles white. No one speaks of the fact that we were a family of five when we were here last, and now we are four. My baby brother is gone forever. None of us speak of the dangers that might still lurk here. Survival comes first. Questions later.

We all flinch when a piece of masonry suddenly clatters down ahead of us. The crack of it hitting the pavement echoes through the ghostly streets. My heart hammers against my ribs, my mouth dry.

Slowly, we continue, the absence of life and sound weighing heavily on us. There is only the crunch of rubble underfoot to mark our passage through this broken place that was once so full of light and laughter. Now, there is only devastation and the faint hope that we can rebuild from this unfathomable loss.

My eyes sting with dust and tears as we round a corner, and our house comes into view. I gasp, my heart dropping. It's little more than a pile of scorched timber and crumbling bricks. Windows shattered, the roof caved in, walls buckled and blackened.

"No," I whisper. This can't be all that's left. Our home, our memories…gone.

My mother lets out a low, agonized moan, sinking to her knees. She reaches out a trembling hand to touch a chunk of metal on our front steps, its edges melted and warped. A small plane that was my baby brother's.

"We'll find a way," my father says, though his voice shakes. "We'll start over."

I blink hard, fighting back the urge to cry. Starting over seems impossible right now. We have no food, no shelter. Winter is coming and everything familiar has been destroyed.

My brother kicks angrily at a piece of timber, his young face hardened. "Those bastards," he mutters.

My father hushes him, glancing around warily. The bombing may have stopped but we don't know who or what still lurks nearby. We need to focus on survival. On finding water, scavenging supplies from the wreckage, and securing basic necessities. The howling emptiness in my stomach is a constant reminder of how much we've lost.

But as I stare at the ruins of our home, I also feel a faint glimmer of hope. The remaining four of us are still alive. We have each other. We can rebuild, even if it seems impossible right now. That is more than Anne had. There is still hope.

I take a deep breath and force myself to look away from the ruins of our home. "There's work to be done if we're going to survive", says my father.

"We should check the other houses," I say quietly. "Maybe we can find supplies."

My father nods. "Good thinking. Let's start with the Cohen's place."

We pick our way carefully through the debris-strewn streets. All around us are the remnants of lives shattered - broken furniture, torn clothing, family photos covered in ash. Each haunted relic makes my heart ache.

When we reach the Cohen's house, their front door is completely gone. Inside, their possessions are strewn about chaotically. I felt like an intruder, rummaging through their kitchen drawers, but we desperately needed anything useful, and Mr. Cohen had already told us to take what we wanted or needed, he would never go back.

"Look, candles!" my brother cries, holding up a half-melted box.

My mother gives him a weary smile. "Good job, sweetheart."

We scour the house, salvaging what we can. Canned goods, blankets, rain barrels, tools. It's amazing how such simple things that were overlooked in the past can become such a source of celebration.

As we step outside, arms laden with supplies, I see our neighbor Avraham across the street. His kind face looks worn, but he waves when he sees us.

"You found some things, good," he says. "Here, I have extra water I can share."

I feel a rush of gratitude. We are in this together. All of us survivors, bonded by hardship, working to rebuild what we've lost. If we support each other, perhaps there will be hope after all.

My mother suggests we visit the community center, where counseling sessions are being held for those impacted by the conflict. She thinks it would help us process our trauma. I don't want to relive it all again, but I know she's right. We need to start healing emotionally too.

At the community center, a kind woman named Ruth helps us open up about our experiences. I tell her about the numbness I've felt since it happened like I'm sleepwalking through each day. She says that's normal, that my mind is protecting itself from painful memories.

"It's okay to feel however you feel," Ruth tells me gently. "There is no right or wrong way to grieve. We just have to get through each moment, one step at a time."

Her words resonate with me. I've been so focused on the practicalities of survival that I haven't let my feelings surface. But now, tears start flowing as I describe seeing our home destroyed. Ruth hands me tissues, listening patiently.

My mother shares her guilt, that she couldn't protect us from the horrors of war. But Ruth reminds her no one could have foreseen this, that she did her best as a mother in impossible circumstances.

I feel lighter after opening up. The pain is still there, but it doesn't consume me as before. For the first time, I have hope that we can heal from this, in time. Even amidst unfathomable loss, there are caring people who want to help us rebuild our lives.

I sift through the rubble, my hands scraping against broken bricks and twisted metal. The air is filled with dust that catches in my throat with each breath. But I don't stop, driven by the need to find something, anything, left of our home.

And then I see it - a glint of silver peeking out from beneath a pile of debris. My heart leaps as I uncover the dented remains of the silver menorah that has been in our family for generations. Tears prick my eyes as I clutch it close, the seven branches still intact.

I bring it inside to where my family is gathered. "Look what I found!" I announce, my voice cracking. Their faces light up at the sight of the menorah, a tangible piece of our past that survived.

That night, we gather around our makeshift dinner table and light the menorah's candles. As the flickering flames illuminate our weary faces, I feel a sense of warmth and hope stir within me. Throughout everything, this menorah remains. Like us, it is damaged but not destroyed. A symbol of resilience and light that can never be extinguished.

My mother squeezes my hand, her eyes glistening. In this simple act of lighting the candles, I feel our family beginning to heal. The road ahead is still uncertain, but at this moment, we have each other. And that gives me the strength to believe we will get through this, together.

I take a deep breath as I stare out across the rubble that was once my home. Though the destruction surrounds me, I know that I cannot let it crush my spirit. The people here need help, and I realize that I can be the one to provide it.

I think of the young children, scared and confused. The elderly, struggling to find shelter and food.

There is so much work to be done. But I am ready to do it.

I walk purposefully over to where a group of volunteers are organizing supplies. "What can I do to help?" I ask, my voice steady. The man looks at me, surprise flickering across his exhausted face. But he quickly recovers and points me toward a stack of boxes.

As I lift and carry, fetching water and distributing food, I feel a sense of purpose begin to take hold. With each small act and each encouraging word, I am making a difference. My hands become calloused, my back sore, but I push on. This work gives me direction, and helping others restores my hope.

By the day's end, I am drained but fulfilled. I gaze up at the setting sun, its rays bathing the land in a warm, golden light. There is beauty here still if you know where to look. I can now start to envision a way forward.

I take one last look around before heading home. The rubble remains, but there are also flickers of life returning. Laughter rings out, candles glow in windows. We are wounded but not defeated. And tomorrow I will return, ready to rebuild once more.

CHAPTER XXIV

My eyes snap open to darkness. The air is thick with smoke that burns my throat. I fumble for my flashlight, hands shaking. The dim light reveals the ruins of my bedroom. The ceiling is partially caved in, and the dresser lies smashed under a pile of rubble. I crawl from my bed, broken glass crunching under my knees. There is a makeshift tent protecting my bed from the elements.

This can't be real. It must be another nightmare. But the blood trickling down my leg is all too real. I make my way to the door, stepping over the remains of my childhood. I pause, listening. Only silence.

I creep into the hall, sweeping my light from side to side. The walls are scorched black, and dust coats the floor like snow. Pictures lie shattered, my smiling face peering up at me. At the end of the hall, a pile of timber blocks the staircase, our escape route.

My light finds Mama's room. The bed is empty, sheets tangled. "Mama?" My voice is small and scratchy. No answer. Panic flutters in my chest. I rush back to my room, to the closet. Dragging out my backpack, I find Anne's diary tucked inside. I clutch it to my chest, taking a deep breath. I have her diary, I have hope. It has served as a talisman against evil.

I hold the diary tightly as I make my way through the ruins of our home. The front door is wide open, late morning light spills inside. Stepping outside, I'm met with a scene from my nightmares.

Where our street once stood is now a wasteland. Buildings are reduced to rubble, and scorched vehicles overturned on the road. The air hangs heavy with dust and smoke, burning my throat with each breath. In the distance, the steady beat of artillery pounds relentlessly. I know this is a flashback. It is not real. The counselors have told me about these, but at the moment it is my only reality.

I stand frozen, struggling to comprehend the devastation. This can't be home. But there, across the street - a lopsided mailbox with the name Goldberg was still visible. This is all that remains.

My legs move automatically, carrying me down the debris-strewn street. I pass remnants of lives interrupted - a child's doll, a shattered picture frame, the tires of a bicycle jutting from a mound of concrete. All a mirage from my damaged psyche.

At the end of the road, a makeshift shelter comes into view. A few familiar faces mill about outside huddled together. I quicken my pace, my heart leaps with momentary relief. I see my mother. Again, I wandered back to my home to sleep amidst the rubble without even realizing it. At first, when this started happening, others would come and get me, but eventually, my mother just put up a cloth canopy over my bed and would sit outside the shelter, watching the remains of our home from a distance and waiting for me to come back to her.

"Rachel!" Mrs. Bailey pulls me into a crushing embrace. Over her shoulder, others gather around, worry and warmth in their tired eyes. For the first time since waking, I felt tears sting my eyes. We're alive. Against all odds, we're alive.

I sit down and open my diary to a fresh page. The blank paper stares up at me, waiting. Where do I even begin?

My pen hovers over the page as I gather my thoughts. I think of Anne, finding strength to write even when death felt imminent. She refused to let fear silence her. I must do the same.

With a slow breath, I start to write. I describe the hollow ache in my chest when I wake each morning, the bone-deep exhaustion of simply existing in this limbo between life and death. I write about how laughter feels foreign now, joy a distant memory.

Yet even in the darkest days, there are pinpricks of light. A gentle hand on my shoulder, a whispered word of comfort, a shared moment of silence - these small acts of humanity sustain me.

My hand trembles as I write of the losses etched into my heart. Friends, neighbors, childhood itself - all gone too soon. But their memories propel me forward. I must live to honor them, to share their truncated stories.

When I finally set down the pen, a wave of relief washes over me. The blank page is no longer empty but filled with a piece of my truth. I have shone a little light into the darkness, as promised.

For now, it is enough.

Diary in hand, I make my way downstairs. Mom is in the kitchen, mechanically washing dishes though our sink ran dry days ago. Dad sits at the table, staring into nothingness.

I clear my throat softly. "I... I wrote some more. About everything that's happened."

Mom's shoulders tense, but she doesn't turn. Dad blinks slowly before meeting my gaze.

"I thought maybe you'd want to read it. It might help." I pause, suddenly unsure. "To understand, I mean."

Dad reaches out and I hand him the diary with trembling fingers. He flips through the pages, emotions flickering across his face. Mom finally turns, wiping her hands on a ragged towel.

"Well?" she asks tightly. Dad just shakes his head, tears in his eyes, at a loss for words.

I feel my face grow hot. What did I expect, that baring my soul would instantly heal our broken family?

But then Dad pulls me into a fierce hug. Mom's eyes glisten with tears as she joins us. No words need to be spoken at this moment. My truth has built a bridge between us. There is hope.

Later, I met my friends at our makeshift shelter. We sit in a circle as I read aloud from my diary. Their faces are rapt, leaning into every word.

When I finish, a heavy silence hangs over us. Then my friend squeezes my hand. "You said what we couldn't," she whispers. Others nod, eyes shining with gratitude. I have given voice to our shared trauma. In speaking my truth, I have helped them face theirs.

I have hope that my diary will travel far, into the hands of strangers hungry for understanding. Every letter I receive, every word of thanks, will be a balm to my weary soul. To know my words can heal, teach, can build empathy - it gives me purpose.

Anne Frank showed me the power of bearing witness. Now I must shine my light, steadily, bravely, so others might find their way through the darkness.

Tonight, I sit alone and open my diary, the pale pages filled with the truth of all I have endured. I trace my fingers over the ink stains, the creases, and the fragments of my shattered childhood preserved within.

This diary has been my sanctuary, my one place of solace amidst the chaos. Anne brought me comfort when all hope seemed lost, her words a lifeline I clung to in my darkest moments. She taught me to keep believing, even when evil prevailed, that goodness still flickered in human hearts.

I write my final entry with a heavy heart, but also deep gratitude.

"Dear Anne,

Thank you for giving me light when all was dark. For inspiring me to find courage when fear reigned. For showing me that even the smallest voice can change the world.

I will honor your memory, and the memories of all who suffered, by choosing love over hate, hope over despair, life over death. Let compassion be my guide, empathy my torch.

With this diary, our stories are intertwined throughout time. I only hope mine can inspire others the way yours did for me. Your spirit lives on, Anne, in the hearts of dreamers who still believe in a better tomorrow.

Gratefully yours forever,

Rachel"

CHAPTER XXV

The sound of birdsong outside my window startles me awake. For a moment, I'm gripped with fear, certain it's the wail of air raid sirens. But no, it's just the chirping of sparrows welcoming the dawn. I let out a shaky breath, trying to calm my racing heart.

The morning light filters into my room, casting everything in a warm glow. It looks so…normal. Peaceful, even. Hard to believe that just a few years ago, these same streets were filled with Hamas, trucks full of men with guns and knives rolling past our barricaded doors. The constant threat of bombardment loomed over us.

I slid out of bed and padded softly to the window. The glass is cracked, spiderweb fissures stretching across its surface, but from a young boy's baseball. No longer does my home show damage from the war that threatened to destroy us just a few short years ago. But beyond, I see people in front of their homes. Blinking up at the clear blue sky like they can't quite believe it's real. Children laugh and skip down the road, carefree once more.

"It's over," I whisper to myself. But the knot in my stomach won't abate. I survived, but so many didn't. Friends and family, all gone in an instant. And here I stand, whole and unharmed. Why was I spared when so many others weren't?

A lump forms in my throat as I turn away from the window. My gaze falls on the diary resting on my desk. Not Anne's diary, not mine from what seems like a lifetime ago, but a new diary. Anne would understand these feelings, I think. My heart aches for her, knowing she never got to see the dawn of peace like I have.

Taking a deep breath, I sit down and open to the first fresh page. I promised I would keep writing, no matter what. My words are all I have to make sense of it all. To honor the lost. Gripping my pen tightly, I am ready to begin…

I pause, staring down at the blank page. Where do I even start? So much has happened, and my thoughts are still a jumble.

But then I remember Anne's words. Her courage in putting her innermost feelings to paper. She was just a girl, like me, but she found a way to be strong when everything around her seemed so dark.

"Dear Anne,"

I start writing.

"I made it. The war is over. I wish so much I could tell you that in person. I wish I could have been there for you when you needed someone. You've been like a sister to me these past years, your words were a light in the blackest of nights."

My hand trembles, and I grip the pen tighter.

"I don't know how to feel right now. I'm relieved it's over but I'm also guilty. Why did I make it out when so many others didn't? What makes me so special?"

Tears blur my vision. I brush them away angrily. Anne never gave up, even when she had lost everything. I have to be strong like her. I must keep going, keep remembering. For Anne. For all those who didn't live to see this day.

Looking out at the rising sun, I make a silent vow. I will live my life in a way that honors those we've lost.

"I'll share your story, Anne, so what happened is never forgotten or repeated. With the light of dawn, there is also hope. If we remember, there's hope we can build a better world."

I close my diary and take a deep breath. The morning air is crisp and clean, the pale sunlight filtering through the trees. For the first time in years, it feels safe to be outside. No more air raid sirens, no more hiding in basements and bomb shelters. We made it.

My friends and family start to emerge from their homes, weary but smiling. Hannah rushes over and gives me a fierce hug. "What a beautiful day, Rachel! Can you believe it?"

I hug her back, a lump in my throat. My best friend. We clung to each other during the darkest times, keeping each other's spirits up with whispered stories and hidden pieces of chocolate, after meeting in the shelter.

The rest of the kibbutz gather in the courtyard, embracing, talking, and laughing. My mother pulls me into her arms, stroking my hair. "My brave girl," she murmurs. "What a beautiful day today is. We are so thankful for this blessing."

My father squeezes my shoulder, his eyes glistening with tears behind his glasses. He went to such lengths to keep us safe, risking his life again and again. I'm overwhelmed with gratitude for my family, my friends, and my community. We went through hell, but we went through it together. I may have been by myself in my safe room, but I was never truly "alone". I am and have always been loved by many. I am blessed.

As we stand there, the sun rises higher, bathing us in golden light. The long night is over. Ahead of us is the monumental task of still rebuilding our lives, our homes are now intact, but there is still much work to be done with our spirits. But we are alive. We made it. As long as we remember, there will always be hope.

I nod and smile along with everyone else, but a heaviness settles in my chest. We survived, but so many didn't. Anne Frank's face appears in my mind - her bright eyes, her playful smile. She was just a girl, like me. Writing gave her comfort amidst the chaos, just as it did for me. But no one came to rescue Anne. No one opened the secret annex door and led her family to safety.

My hands tremble as I clutch my diary, Anne's words echoing in my mind:

"In spite of everything, I still believe that people are really good at heart." (Frank, 1991)

Did she still believe that in her final days in the camp? When she needed saving the most, and no one came? A tear rolls down my cheek. I quickly brush it away before anyone notices.

Later that night, I sit on my bed, unable to sleep. The neighborhood is silent, and everyone else is lost in dreams. I open my diary with a shaky hand and begin to write.

"My dearest Anne,

I'm sorry. I'm sorry no one was there to help you. That while I survived, you did not..."

I stop, overcome. It's so unfair. Anne was just as deserving of life as I am. More tears fall, splashing on the page. I roughly wipe them away, smearing the ink.

When the tears finally cease, I continue writing. I write about my guilt, my anger at the injustice of it all. Anne deserved to see the sunrise after the long night, to rebuild her life, to fulfill her dreams. My heart aches for her, for all those we've lost. I vow to honor them by living fully, and by sharing their stories. I will remember.

I stare at the page, my mind spinning. How could such horror have happened? Why was I spared when so many others were not? It all seems so senseless, so random.

Fate is fickle. Life is fragile. In one moment, everything can change. I think of how quickly lives were upended when the Nazis arrived. I think about the constant fear and uncertainty that now defines our existence because of Hamas. They are quiet now, but for how long?

We have endured so much. Lost so much. I glance around at the other houses, imagining the people that I know and love asleep in their beds. We are the lucky ones, but at what cost?

There are some moments the mind cannot comprehend, wounds too deep to heal. All we can do is pick up the pieces and try to rebuild. Try to make sense of it all.

I grip my pen tightly, flooded with emotion.

"We must honor the dead by bearing witness. By telling their stories so the truth is not silenced. Evil prevails when good men stand by and do nothing.

The horrors of the Holocaust must not be forgotten. We will speak out, write, remember. Keep the memories alive so history does not repeat itself. Humans have a duty to one another. I have a duty to you, Anne, to share your story with the world.

Your voice will not be stifled. Your spirit will live on. This, I vow with all my heart as I sit here in my darkened bedroom, the memories of suffering always close in the shadows. We will go on."

I stare down at the empty pages, unsure where to even begin. How can I put into words the incomprehensible things I've witnessed? The depth of cruelty humans are capable of.

My hand trembles as I start to write.

"I close my eyes, picturing your face, Anne. Your courage inspires me. Gives me strength. If you could endure with such spirit, then so must I.

We have survived against all odds. Reclaimed our lives from the edge of oblivion. Though we are broken, our people endure. The Nazis tried to extinguish your flame, but you refused to be extinguished. Your words have lived on.

There is hope. If we remember, if we rebuild, evil has not won. Your spirit lives on in me, Anne. I will tell your story to the world.

Love,

Rachel

The pen falls from my fingers. I am spent, emotionally and physically. But also renewed with purpose. My people are bloodied but unbowed. Anne's memory gives me the courage to face each new day.

I will continue writing, dear friend. My words are a flicker of light in the darkness. Together, our voices will ensure the truth prevails. Forever.

EPILOGUE

I sit inside my rebuilt home in our kibbutz, staring down at the letter in my hands. It is many years later and I am a mother now. My daughter, playing in the courtyard, a carefree 13 year old on her last birthday. The paper is worn and creased many times over. My name is written across the front in neat, looping handwriting.

With trembling fingers, I unfold it and begin to read again as I have so many times before.

"Dear Rachel,

I don't know if this will ever reach you. I hope it does. I found your diary when I was staying at a shelter. Someone had donated a box of books and there it was - your story.

I couldn't put it down. I read the whole thing in one night, crying and laughing and feeling not so alone anymore. Your words gave me hope during the darkest time in my life. You made me believe I could survive, just like you did.

I know it might seem strange, but I feel like I know you now. Your diary lets me see inside your mind and your heart. You're so much braver than me. Even when you were scared or hurt, you never gave up.

I wish I could be as strong as you. I'm trying, little by little. On days when it seems too hard, I think of you finding light even in the darkness. You inspire me, Rachel.

I hope we will get to meet someday. I'd love to tell you in person how your story changed my life. For now, thank you for sharing your diary with the world. You've given us all such a gift. Don't ever stop writing.

With admiration,

Clara"

I read the letter again and again, Clara's words blurring on the page. She said my story changed her life. I think of the tattered blue diary tucked away in my bag, now in the back of my closet, filled with my innermost thoughts. Did those private words really help someone?

At first, it's almost unbelievable. Me, make a difference? I was just a girl trying to survive, to block out the fear. But Clara's letter is proof - my story connected with her.

Maybe, just maybe, my words were more than just a diary. They turned into a light in the darkness for others, just as Anne's were for me.

I feel the weight of this, the gravity of what Clara's letter means. It's both wonderful and awful. My story kept someone going, yet so many didn't make it. Survivor's guilt wells up inside me, even these many years later, threatening to swallow me whole.

I take a deep breath, steadying myself. Clara is out there waiting, hoping. If I can help just one person feel less alone, then I must keep writing. My words are no longer just for me now - they're for Clara, for Anne, for all those silenced too soon.

I carefully tuck the letter into my bag beside the diary. Later today, I will write to Clara. I will tell her she gives me hope too. For now, I will do what I can to shine a little light in this darkness.

ABOUT THE AUTHOR

Tammy L. Brown is an accomplished author hailing from the picturesque town of Toccoa, Georgia, nestled at the base of the foothills of the Blue Ridge Mountains. Her writing journey has been shaped by a diverse range of experiences and influences. In this poignant and emotionally charged book, Tammy explores the life-altering impact of Anne Frank's diary on a young girl in modern-day Israel, who found solace and strength within its pages, inspiring her to document her own time of conflict and adversity.

Tammy's life is deeply intertwined with the military, as she is married to a disabled combat veteran. Their shared experiences, sacrifices, and resilience have fueled her passion for storytelling and connecting with her readers on a profound level. During their time stationed in Bavaria, Germany, Tammy and her husband visited Dachau, a concentration camp with a haunting history that left an indelible mark on her. This experience deepened her commitment to shedding light on the power of literature and human resilience, which is evident in this extremely moving work.

Tammy L. Brown's writing not only brings history to life but also serves as a testament to the enduring strength of the human spirit. Her ability to craft narratives that resonate with readers, drawing from personal experiences and a profound sense of empathy, makes her a notable and compassionate voice in the world of literature.